THE LADY V

Jan Mark has won many prizes for her books, including the Carnegie Medal (twice), the Penguin Guardian Award and the Observer Teenage Fiction Prize. Her many titles include *Taking the Cat's Way Home* and *They Do Things Differently There* (shortlisted for the 1994 Whitbread Children's Novel Award), as well as the Walker picture books *Fur*, *Strat and Chatto* (Winner of the 1990 Mother Goose Award), *This Bowl of Earth* and *Lady Long-Legs*. Jan Mark lives in Oxford.

Books by the same author

Picture books

Fur
Strat and Chatto
The Tale of Tobias
The Midas Touch

For younger readers

The Snow Maze
Taking the Cat's Way Home
Lady Long-Legs

For older readers

The Eclipse of the Century
God's Story
Mr Dickens Hits Town
Nothing To Be Afraid Of
The Sighting
They Do Things Differently There
Thunder and Lightnings

THE LADY
WITH
IRON BONES

JAN MARK

WALKER BOOKS
AND SUBSIDIARIES
LONDON • BOSTON • SYDNEY

First published 2000 by Walker Books Ltd
87 Vauxhall Walk, London SE11 5HJ

This edition published 2001

2 4 6 8 10 9 7 5 3 1

Text © 2000 Jan Mark
Cover illustration © 2000 Christian Birmingham

This book has been typeset in Sabon

Printed in Great Britain by
Cox & Wyman Ltd, Reading, Berkshire

British Library Cataloguing in Publication Data:
a catalogue record for this book is
available from the British Library

ISBN 0-7445-7884-1

For Wendy Boase

CHAPTER ONE

In the middle of the Lord's Prayer, Ellen looked at Kasey Carter and saw that she was actually praying. Everyone was going through the motions as usual, hands together, heads down, even if they were passing football stickers. But Kasey was really doing it, fingers clenched under her chin, lips moving.

Ellen could see that she was not saying, "Give us this day our daily bread", but the same thing over and over, something beginning with P.

"Please. Please. Please. Please. Please."

"Amen." Everyone stopped as if a switch had been thrown; hands dropped, necks straightened, eyes opened. Kasey saw Ellen looking at her and the last "Please" turned into an unmistakable "Push off", with a face to match.

Ellen made a face back. Kasey was her best

friend, she did not mean any harm by it. At least, Ellen hoped she didn't. Still, best friends shared secrets and Kasey had not told Ellen about anything that would set her off praying like that in public. Audworth Primary was a Church of England school but people went there because it was the only one in the village. Children whose parents felt strongly about it went into the town where there were more schools to choose from.

They all swivelled to the left to file out. Kasey was behind Ellen and there was no chance to turn and say anything because Mrs Bean was standing at the end of their row, watching for people to do just that – especially watching for Kasey who could rouse Mrs Bean to wrath just by looking at her. Ellen tried to remember if Kasey had seemed particularly troubled about anything lately. The last time Kasey had been worried was about SATs and they had all been so nervous that Ellen would not have noticed Kasey especially. And Kasey was a frowning, brooding person at the best of times, with plenty to brood about, given to muttering under her breath so that teachers thought she was sulking. But just now she had not been muttering; that had been real praying; *Please. Please. Please*; her fingers so tightly clasped that the nails had gone white.

"*Move*, Ellen," Mrs Bean said crossly, and Ellen sprang forward as Kasey piled into her from behind.

"What you standing there for?" Kasey mumbled, and "Stop whispering, Kasey," Mrs Bean said, and Ellen realized that she had been so busy wondering that she had missed the command to follow Year 5.

"I saw you gawping in assembly," Kasey said truculently at break.

"Sorry," Ellen said. Saying "Sorry" to Kasey came as naturally as saying "Bless you" when somebody sneezed. You didn't need to have done anything to feel sorry for, it was simply a way in to the next sentence. "I just wondered what you were praying about."

"None of your business," Kasey growled, but Ellen knew that Kasey must have wanted her to ask or she would not have raised the subject. They walked on round the edge of the playing field, eating their crisps.

At last Kasey spluttered, through a mouthful of crumbs, "Kray's gone off after his dad."

"When?"

"Yesterday. While I was at school. He left a note, but Mum had to wait for me to come home because I'm the only one who can read his writing. Here."

Kray Carter was seventeen and if he had been Ellen's brother she would have been glad to have him out of the way. He was moody and unpredictable like Kasey and, being six

9

feet tall, alarming with it. Her little brother Macauley was eighteen months and had not started talking yet. They were a silent family.

Kray's farewell note was written in pencil on the back of an Anadin packet, unfolded flat.

"He says he's gone to Birmingham to find his dad and see if he can get a job and he can't stick it round here any more. I didn't tell Mum that bit. He knew I'd be the one to read it. He wouldn't want to upset her. Well, not more than going off to Birmingham would. You know how she is."

Ellen did know. "Were you praying he'd come back, then?"

"He can go to Newcastle for all *I* care," Kasey said, brutally. Newcastle was where people went on *EastEnders*, the edge of the known Universe. Then she sighed and her shoulders slumped. "But Mum's going on like he's died. She goes spare if he just stays out all night. You still got two crisps left."

Ellen handed one over.

"Won't do any good, though. Never does."

"You tried it before?"

"With SATs. I asked and asked for level 6."

Ellen thought that she had been pushing it a bit and passed over the second crisp.

"Don't go mad," Kasey said, but she took it anyway. "And after we'd done it I asked for level 5 – or 4."

"But you couldn't change it – not after

you'd done it."

"God could've," Kasey said. "But he never."

It did not occur to Ellen to use prayer-time in assembly for cadging favours. They often prayed for world peace, which was only reasonable, but given the way the news usually turned out that was more like hoping, or even wishing. From time to time she would find herself whispering, "Oh, please let it happen," or, more often, "Please, don't let it happen," but not *to* anyone in particular. Things went right ahead and happened, or did not, no matter what she wanted.

On Saturdays and Wednesdays she stood with her fingers crossed and one of them touching wood, while Mum filled out the lottery ticket, and again when the numbers were picked on television, but the only time they had won more than ten pounds she had been ill in bed with tonsillitis, not thinking about the lottery at all and only touching the duvet cover.

"Well, I expect Kray'll come back," she said, as the whistle blew for the end of break, "specially if he doesn't find a job."

She realized how tactless this was when Kasey said, "I never prayed he wouldn't find a job. I just don't want him to find it in Birmingham."

It was so easy to say the wrong thing to

11

Kasey and most people did every time they spoke to her, from Mrs Bean down to Marsha and Emily who shared their table in class. Emily made a point of saying the wrong thing on purpose. Her mother was the school secretary and Emily knew more than was good for her about other people's business, passing it to anyone who would listen, or could not help hearing. Kasey was an easy target. "Kray's only her half-brother. His dad went off … now *her* dad's gone … her mum's depressed … that baby's backward."

Depressed; backward. Emily made them sound like shameful things to be. "Ellen's *Kasey's* friend." She made that sound shameful too, but Ellen was not ashamed.

"What do you see in that girl?" Ellen's mum asked once, after one of Kasey's rare visits. Ellen had to take time out to think about that, and came to the conclusion that she liked Kasey because Kasey liked her. Kasey liked very few people, so it was almost an honour.

Several times during the rest of the day Ellen glanced across the table and saw Emily watching Kasey, who sat, head down, lips moving, "Please, please, please," like someone pressing the redial button on a telephone; *Perhaps I'll get through this time*.

"Try it in church," Ellen suggested, towards the end of the last lesson. It was art and they were making prints. "It might work

12

better in there."

"Why?" Kasey said. "God's everywhere, isn't he? That's what they're always telling us."

"What's church for, then?" Ellen said. "It's his house, isn't it? He must go home sometimes."

"Mum'll worry if I'm late. She's worried enough over Kray and that. And someone'll have to get Mac's tea."

"I didn't mean go to a service thingy. It'll only take a minute."

St Mary's Church was close to the school, across The Street at the top of Bell Lane. Neither of them went home that way, but if they left the moment the last lesson ended, as Kasey always did anyway, they would lose only a few minutes, not enough to be noticed.

Ellen had not been in the church since Easter, and had not expected to be there again before Harvest Festival. In fact, by October, she and Kasey would be at the big school, in town. If the big school did things in church it would not be St Mary's but the parish church that you could see from the fields, with pinnacles on its high tower.

St Mary's tower was short and squat and its clock was always six minutes fast. Ellen and Kasey sprinted up the side path between the yew hedges and in at the south door. The church was kept locked most of the time but on Friday evenings there was a choir practice and the door was unbolted. They tiptoed inside and crept across the flagstones to the strip of red carpet that ran up the aisle. The flower-arrangers had been at work – there must be a wedding tomorrow – and Ellen stayed to sniff at the roses and Shasta daisies, but Kasey walked boldly towards the altar and opened the gate in the communion rail.

Ellen ran after her. "You're not supposed to go in there."

"Can if I like. Want to get up close," Kasey said. "You don't have to watch."

Ellen retreated to a choir stall at a safe distance near the rood screen, next to the stained-glass window where Jesus was feeding the five thousand. Kasey knelt down on the step right in front of the altar.

Ellen knew it was the feeding of the five thousand because Jesus had the barley loaves under his arm and was holding up the two small fishes by their tails, like a man with a winning hand at poker. The window was not large and the five thousand were represented by seven people at the front, with faces, and then rows of bumps like cobblestones. Ellen counted heads, as she always did when sitting in sight of this particular window. She never managed to make it come out at the same number.

At Harvest Festivals there was always a

14

giant marrow displayed on this window-sill. Ellen wondered if they had Harvest Festivals at secondary schools. Perhaps they didn't have Carol Services either, or Nativity Plays; no imitation pillar boxes in the front hall for posting Christmas cards. She had had her last Easter, her last Harvest Festival, her last Christmas at St Mary's. This might be the last time she ever sat here, counting the five thousand.

At the altar Kasey was getting to her feet. She closed the gate in the communion rail behind her, and gave a last *Or else* look at the altar.

"Come on," she said to Ellen as she passed the choir stalls, never pausing to look at the window. "We're late."

"*You're* late," Ellen retorted quietly, following her. Mum would not be home for at least another hour. So long as Ellen was in before she was, she did not fuss. Kasey had to get all the way to the bottom of Church Road and along Water Lane to reach The Estate, but Ellen lived so near to the school that she could see the corner of her roof from the end of the playing field. At this time of year she could stroll. It was different in winter, those few weeks before Christmas when she almost had to race the sunset home.

"See you Monday," Kasey said at the end of the red carpet.

"What about tomorrow?"

"Can't come out and leave Mac with Mum, *can* I?" Kasey said. "Unless Kray comes back. 'Course, if anyone's listening—" she turned and bellowed down the echoing nave— *"he'll be back when I get home!"* She hauled the heavy door open and took off at a run, through the porch and down the path between the yews. Ellen saw her turn left at the end, down The Street. She was going to take a short cut across the fields, which would make her mother worry even more if she knew about it, if she had any worry to spare for Kasey. Kasey was forbidden to go into the fields alone, like most people at school. Ellen was not one of them.

Ellen and Mum lived in a flat. It was not one of a block like the flats on The Estate, but the top half of an ordinary house in Church Road. Downstairs lived the Walcotts who came and went through the front door. They had a back door too, that led into their share of the garden behind the house. Ellen and Mum's door was at the side, with their own bell beside it and a printed notice that read *J. and E. Downie*, which was them, Jessica and Ellen. The door opened into a lobby with stairs that ran up straight into their kitchen, carved from the old front master bedroom.

They had their own bit of garden too, beyond the Walcotts', with a narrow path to reach it that ran between the Walcotts' larch-lap fence and the hedge that belonged to Mrs Sayer next door. Her garden was three times bigger than the Downies' and the Walcotts' put together.

At the end of the garden lay the fields, and in the fields stood the Blasted Oak.

The village was hardly a village any more, the town was creeping round it year by year, estate by estate, but the fields still lay at the heart of it; allotments, the Rugby Club pitch, the school playing field, a little swing park over by The Estate where Kasey lived, and an open space that belonged to no one, crossed by a footpath. Other mothers sucked their teeth and muttered because Ellen's mother let Ellen play alone in the fields. You never knew what might happen.

"What might happen?" Ellen had asked Mum.

"You might go off with someone."

"But you always say I mustn't."

Mum had raised her eyebrows as if amazed to think that Ellen might actually refrain from doing something because she had been told not to do it. "Suppose you were attacked?"

"People would see – there's houses all round. And the allotments."

"Just don't ever go out of sight of the flat, then," Mum had said.

This was fine by Ellen because there was only one place that she wanted to go and that was the Blasted Oak, which was well within sight of the flat. It was a tree that had been struck by lightning, years ago, and split in two. Now there was nothing left but a hollow jagged stump, her special place where she could sit, private and hidden. She could see people coming in any direction, long before they could see her, and if anyone looked like trouble, she had her emergency exit.

To get round to her front gate in Church Road would mean a dash along the footpath beside Mrs Sayer's garden, over the stile and up the hill. She could imagine being pursued, flagging on that steep bit, legs trembling, fingers grabbing at her shoulder, but it need never happen. Directly opposite the Blasted Oak was Mrs Sayer's back fence. It was a proper fence with upright planks, sturdy and creosoted, not like the Walcotts' larch-lap job from B & Q or the Downies' chain-link. But ten planks in from the boundary hedge were two loose ones. Ellen had first noticed them from the Blasted Oak and moved them aside to find out what lay beyond. It had not taken her long to work out that she was in next door's garden and that to her right was a gap under the hedge where she could cut through to her own.

So for a while those loose boards in Mrs Sayer's fence had been kept in reserve, a bolt hole, a safety-hatch, if ever she needed to make a quick getaway. But they had soon become her regular way home and, eventually, her regular way out, too. Now she always used them, stooping under the hedge and through the hinterland of Mrs Sayer's rubbish heap. Although she was fairly sure that Mrs Sayer could not see her, she never hung about these days but always dived catercorner, straight for the loose planks.

There were still fifty minutes left before Mum would be back. Ellen let herself in with the key that she kept hanging round her neck, ran up the stairs and dropped her schoolbag in the kitchen. Then she came down, locked up again and went quietly along the path between the Walcotts' garden and Mrs Sayer's, until she reached the room-sized patch at the end which belonged to her and Mum, where her secret tunnel ran under the hedge. In less than half a minute she was through the garden and out in the fields.

Ellen sat on the cushiony grass at the base of the oak stump, leaning back against the curve of the soft, charred heartwood, as if she were in an enormous armchair. It was a long time since she had played here. Sometimes she brought a book but usually she just sat, hearing the voices of people passing on the footpath, enjoying the thought that they did not know she was there, so close and unseen, listening for the church clock to strike five, six minutes fast, giving her time to streak through the fence and get indoors in time to put the kettle on before Mum arrived.

Then she would make tea while Mum checked her e-mail. She and Mum always had a cup of tea together and exchanged news. Ellen's only real news today was that Kray had gone to Birmingham to find his dad, but Ellen did not feel like passing this on. The news would be all over The Estate soon enough, and then leak out to the rest of the village, but for now it was Kasey's private sorrow. She had not said to Ellen, "Don't tell anybody," or, more Kasey-like, "Don't feel you've got to let everyone else know," but as Kasey never told other people anything, Ellen always kept her confidences as secrets.

On those days when Kasey was late for registration and Mrs Bean asked, "Does anyone know where Kasey is?", Ellen did know. But she never piped up, "Miss, her mum's depressed again and she's got to look after Macauley." Someone else, just guessing, was sure to do that.

CHAPTER TWO

Ellen ran into Kasey unexpectedly on Sunday afternoon, on the way home from buying milk at the Co-op. They always ran out of milk on Sundays because she and Mum sat around all morning looking at the papers and drinking coffee. Ellen did not find the papers very interesting and coffee was not her favourite drink, but she loved that time when she and Mum were together with no work or homework, shopping or cleaning to worry about, just the peaceful routine of having no routine. Even running out of milk was part of it. Mum could have ordered an extra pint from the milkman on Saturday because she knew they always needed it.

Ellen did not recognize Kasey at first. She thought it was a grown-up slouching along behind the buggy, steering it with one hand. Then she recognized the baby as Macauley, looked harder at the grown-up and saw Kasey. Although they were in the same year at school they had been born at opposite ends of it, Ellen in October and Kasey the following August, but Kasey looked older and seemed it. She had older things to think about.

Ellen waved and crossed the road. Kasey halted and leaned against the bus stop, pushing the buggy back and forth with her foot.

"He yells if we stop moving," Kasey said. "Goes right through you, like toothache." She sounded grown-up too, like one of the mothers who waited outside the school to collect an infant.

"Any news?" Ellen said.

"Naaah. Didn't work. Knew it wouldn't."

Ellen guessed what she was talking about. "How's your mum?"

"Hasn't got up yet, has she?" Kasey said. "That's why I've got *him*." She gave the buggy a jerk and Macauley's head bounced. "He's having a mood … screaming … I don't know, maybe it's his teeth."

Macauley's head appeared round the side of the buggy, staring owl-eyed at Ellen.

"Mew," he said.

"Cat?" Ellen looked all around, hopefully. A nice friendly cat would make Macauley happy and perhaps even cheer Kasey up.

Macauley pointed and made grabbing motions towards Ellen. "Mew. *Mew*."

"He's talking," Ellen said, excitedly. She crouched by the buggy. "Say it again, Mac."

"Meeow?" Kasey said, scornfully. "He's meant to say *words*."

Macauley stiffened and began to turn red with frustration.

"*Mew!*"

Ellen held up the carton. "Is that it, Mac?"

"Mew." Macauley grinned and bounced enthusiastically.

"He's saying *milk*," Ellen said. "His first word. Clever Mac. Nearly there. Say milk. Miiiiilk."

"Mew."

"What d'you want to show him that for?" Kasey said, tiredly. "Now we'll have to give him some." She fossicked in the string bag that hung from the buggy handle and took out a feeding bottle and teat. Macauley had not mastered the art of cups yet. He grabbed the bottle, plugged himself in and reclined in lordly fashion, eyes closing as the level of the liquid went down in alarming surges.

"Wasn't he meant to drink it, then?"

"Not yet, not all of it – I'll never get it away from him now," Kasey complained. "It's like pulling up horse radish, getting a bottle away from him. I tell him, he'll end up a wino on the streets, swigging antifreeze. *Woncha?*" she said threateningly to Macauley, who belched and gulped without pausing, circular breathing like an oboist.

"Get him some more."

"Haven't got any dosh; have you?"

"No, I only had enough for this. We could give him some," Ellen said. "I know, come home and he can have some orange juice."

"Mum doesn't like him drinking orange, not with all those Euro things in it. Nah—" she gave the buggy another shove— "Mum wouldn't notice if he drank washing-up liquid. *I* don't like him drinking squash. There's all things bad for his teeth and stuff."

"It's not squash, it's juice, we get it from the milkman."

"In glass bottles?"

"Yes. Real juice."

"All right, then," Kasey said. "Thanks." They set off at a brisk pace, then she slumped again.

"What'll your mum say? She doesn't like me."

"Yes she does."

"She doesn't," Kasey said, without rancour.

"Only 'cause she doesn't know you. She doesn't *not* like you, she just … doesn't, well, *like* you."

Kasey understood. There were no flies on Kasey, whatever the SATs results might or might not have proved.

When they had first been friends, too little to go out alone, they had made plans for when they were older; dropping in on each other after school, going to town, to cafés, clubs, shopping trips, visits to London, even. Then Macauley had arrived, Mr Carter had left. Nothing was said, but Ellen went round to Kasey's only once or twice; Kasey came to Ellen's once or twice. It felt uncomfortable. They were school friends. On Fridays they parted at Ellen's gate and talked idly about meeting over the weekend, then each went home to the place where the other did not belong.

Ellen pressed on, "We could take Mac to the swing park after."

Kasey looked almost eager. "I'll keep him out till he's tired. He can go straight to bed when he gets in. He's missing Kray, though."

Ellen supposed that, if a house needed a man, Kray was the man of the Carters' house, even though his name was Robson. Who would stand up for them now?

By the time they reached Church Road Macauley had finished his milk and was sucking deeply on the empty bottle like a man whose pipe will not draw.

"That's right, fill yourself with wind." Kasey parked the buggy by the gate and began prising the bottle out of Macauley's fingers. "*More* drink, Mac. Soon." Macauley looked unconvinced but started to let go.

"Come on in."

"No. You just rinse out the bottle and fill it with juice." Kasey, unsure of her welcome, or sure of her unwelcome, stood by the hedge where she thought she could not be seen from the front windows.

Mum was in the kitchen when Ellen came up the stairs. She looked at the bottle. "Where'd you get that from?"

"It's Mac's – Macauley Carter."

"What are you doing with it?"

"He's finished all his milk. Can we give him some orange?"

"We?"

"Me and Kasey – save her going home again."

Mum took the bottle and held it up to the window. "When was this last washed?"

"Not Kasey's fault ... just ... only a bit of orange..." Ellen mumbled.

Mum switched on the kettle, unscrewed the teat from the bottle, put all the pieces in a jug and poured boiling water on them.

"Not that that'll do a lot of good," she remarked, dropping a globule of washing-up liquid into the bottle, shaking it to a froth, rinsing and rinsing again.

"Mum, hurry up. Kasey's waiting."

"Won't kill her to wait a bit longer. Fancy giving a baby—"

"He's *not* a baby, he's eighteen months," Ellen burst out. "He eats all sorts of cack, you know what little kids do, mud and grass and

26

stuff. That bottle won't hurt him. Kasey won't even let him drink squash because of the additives."

Mum looked surprised. "She won't?"

"No. You're not being fair. I wouldn't know how to look after him like she does. You wouldn't make me if he was ours, would you? You wouldn't *let* me."

"No," Mum said, sadly. She took the one hundred per cent pure orange juice out of Ellen's hand and carefully filled Macauley's bottle. "Does she let him have chocolate?"

"Yes, but I don't think she thinks he should."

Mum put the juice back in the fridge and took out two Kit-Kat bars, chill and brittle, just the way Ellen liked them.

"He can have a bit of yours," she said.

"One for Kasey?"

"Why not? Where is she taking him, the swing park?"

"I thought I'd go too."

Mum looked out of the kitchen window, where Kasey's head was clearly visible above the Walcotts' front hedge. Macauley's outraged shrieks were loud and piercing, like an ambulance siren, and his crimson face suddenly lurched into view over Kasey's shoulder.

"Oh, for God's sake," Mum said, half to herself. Then she opened the window and called, "Kasey!"

Kasey looked up and round, startled. "Yes?" And she looked wary, as if she thought Mum was going to start yelling complaints about the row that Mac was making. It was much more likely that Mrs Walcott would do that if they didn't shut him up quickly. The Walcotts had screaming rows at all hours, but put notes through the letterbox if Ellen made too much noise running upstairs after school. Mum said they only did it to make her feel guilty for not being there.

"Bring him up here," Mum said to Kasey. "You can leave the buggy by the side door."

Kasey looked even more startled. Ellen leaned against the closed half of the window and beckoned. She could hardly elbow her way out beside Mum and shout, "It's all right, she won't bite."

Kasey waved and appeared in the gateway, backing up the steps and pulling the buggy with one hand while trying to balance Macauley on her free arm. Mac, scenting possibilities for hell-raising, began to writhe like a trapped octopus.

"Go down and help her," Mum said. "I'll sort out his nibs for half an hour. You two can eat your chocolate in peace. Why not sit in the garden?"

Ellen ran down the stairs and met Kasey as she reached the top of the garden steps.

"Got the orange?"

"No. Mum says she'll look after him for a bit while we go and sit in the garden."

"What's she want to do that for?" Kasey, who had relaxed for a second, sprang back into her usual wariness. "He probably needs changing. I got a spare nappy in the bag. Get it out, I'll do it before we go up."

"Don't be stupid," Ellen said. "She knows how to change a nappy. She knows what babies are like. She won't expect him to be clean."

"I bet she said something about that bottle," Kasey said, but she stamped on the buggy's brake and followed Ellen up the stairs. Mac, still screaming, tried to clamber over her shoulder and dive head first into the lobby.

Mum was waiting at the top with outstretched arms and plucked him away from his suicide attempt. Mac, feeling himself held by someone big enough to balance him, stopped struggling and stared at Mum's face with beady eyes, weighing her up.

"Pick on someone your own size," Mum told him. "You two go and eat your chocolate and I'll babysit – if that's all right with you, Kasey?" she added, seeing Kasey's suspicious squint.

"Yeah … fine. Thanks." Kasey, trying not to growl, could only whisper. "I've got a spare nappy here. He might…"

"Of course he will," Mum said. "You know

what babies are like. He probably took a dump the minute you changed the last one."

Kasey smiled, and her face looked almost lumpy as her mouth pushed it into an unaccustomed shape.

Mum had little time for digging, weeding and pruning so the patch of garden was mostly grass with a few low bushes in narrow beds around the edge. It looked its best in spring when for three or four weeks the bulbs that lay hidden for the rest of the year burst out into yellow daffodils and red tulips, blue grape hyacinths and every colour of crocus. There was no sign of them now but Kasey looked at it all with approval. Her own back garden was much longer and wider, but it was wall-to-wall grass that had grown into prickly tussocks, although it must once have been a lawn. She sat upright, with her legs stretched out straight in front, nibbling at the Kit-Kat to make it last as long as possible.

"Fancy keeping chocolate in the fridge."

"Don't you like it?"

"'Course I do. It's like ice cream, only no cream. You ever eaten fish fingers straight out the freezer? Fish creams. That's what this is like. Where's that go to?"

"What?"

"That tunnel thing."

"That's where I cut through to the fields.

You can't get out the end of this garden because the council put up chain-link, but Next Door's got a fence. I go in and out through that."

"Cool," Kasey said. "Let's have a look." She crunched up the last piece of chocolate almost without noticing and headed for the hedge. Ellen, alarmed, darted ahead of her and went through the gap first. Kasey had not taken in that they would be trespassing and had not thought of the precautions that Ellen always took, checking to make sure that Mrs Sayer was nowhere about. If Kasey went rampaging through the hole first they might run straight into Mrs Sayer.

Ellen had been crossing the end of Mrs Sayer's garden for so long that she scarcely saw it any more. Always in a hurry she was down on her knees and under the hedge in one movement, on her feet in a stooping run in another, and through the fence in a third. Today, as she reached the fence, she glanced back and saw that Kasey was still kneeling in the gap beneath the hedge, peering round like a nervous rabbit emerging from its burrow.

"Don't stop there. Hurry up. Someone'll see us."

"No, they won't." Kasey twitched her hair free of the hedge thorns and crawled out slowly. "If we can't see the windows, they can't see us – people looking out, I mean." She stood upright, which Ellen never dared to do, and craned her neck. "I can't see over all that, even on tiptoes."

Ellen straightened up cautiously. Kasey was right. Since she had first started cutting through the garden things had changed. The apple tree was wreathed in wild hops whose big rough leaves concealed the dappled view that she had once glimpsed through the branches. Beyond it stood a thicket of Japanese knotweed like a bamboo stockade that had sprouted, and a clump of pampas grass raised its plumy feather dusters three metres in the air. A rose bush, once pruned close and stocky, flung long spiny vines against the sky, and the roses themselves, which Ellen remembered as being plump and round, were fragile handfuls of petals striped white and red, like peppermints. The ivy which had been on its way up the fence had now reached the top and doubled back, hanging in long swags, and a couple of elder bushes, that had got started on their own, stood almost as high as the fence. Where once she had been able to look through and between the leaves and stems, across the lawn – so much greener than their own grass – past the rose bushes that bordered the path, and the flower beds, there was now a solid green screen. Even the cinder path which wound round the rubbish heap had vanished under a mat of couch grass and chickweed. Ellen could just make out where the abandoned stepladder lay, by its contours, but that was only because she knew where to look. Something else was hidden too; the lady with iron bones.

Kasey stood knee-deep among the grasses and wild poppies, gazing open-mouthed, like someone who had been going to Tesco, taken a different route and found herself in heaven.

"Oh, it's lovely," she said. "It's beautiful. I've never seen ... do you play here?"

Kasey rarely talked about playing; still more rarely did she do it. Kasey usually had more pressing concerns, but now she was smiling again. "You could make dens – or a *house*, a little *house*. No one would know. You could live here." She began darting from bush to tree to fence, fingering the roses, stroking the apples, lifting the ivy stems and letting them drop from her hands.

"They smell lovely, these big green and yellow ones." She cracked a curling leathery leaf with her thumbnail and inhaled. "Have a sniff of that."

Ellen caught a thick, pungent perfume, not at all what you would expect from ivy. All the time she had been passing those leaves and never knew they could smell like that.

"Come on, we mustn't stay here."

"Why not?"

"Why d'you think? It's somebody's garden.

33

Mrs Sayer, I told you."

"Well, if she doesn't want you in it she should mend her fence," Kasey said. "Anyway, she can't care much about this bit, letting it get all overgrown. You can tell she never comes down here."

"She comes down to the rubbish heap," Ellen said.

"Well, not much, she can't. She never comes round this part, I bet. You'd be able to see marks in the grass."

Kasey was right. For the first time it occurred to Ellen that the reason why she so seldom saw Mrs Sayer these days was that Mrs Sayer spent less time gardening. The lawn and the flower beds were still cared for, but the part that was out of sight was going back to nature.

"It's like Tarzan in the jungle. You could swing on these." Kasey was sweeping aside the fronds of ivy with the backs of her fingers, as if playing a harp, letting them swing and swish back into place, like curtains. "Ow!" She stopped and flinched, rattling her hand in the air to shake away the pain.

"What happened?"

"There's something under here." More carefully she hooked up the ivy stems and peered into the dark, spider-haunted cavity behind them, and there, still standing as Ellen had last seen her, with that close and secret smile, was the lady with iron bones.

CHAPTER THREE

She was not quite as Ellen recalled. Pale ivy stems with tiny sun-starved yellow starfish leaves were beginning to climb up her drapery. They came away with a muted rasping as Kasey dislodged their grip.

"Careful." Ellen put out a steadying hand. "She's ever so heavy."

The statue rocked warningly on its pedestal as Kasey withdrew. "Who is she?"

"I don't know. I just call her the lady with iron bones."

Ellen had always called her that, from the time when she had first slipped under the hedge and come face to face with her, standing askew and abandoned against Mrs Sayer's back fence behind the rubbish heap. In those days she had been much closer to Ellen in height. Her hair was pulled back in a bun, although hard little curls framed her forehead and neck, her head tilted to one side as she looked up from the shell that she held in both hands. She wore a kind of loose robe, clasped on the shoulders with round brooches. The robe fell open at one side and her bent left leg was bare – what remained of it. She was made of concrete around a metal armature and the concrete had broken away below the knee, exposing the iron shin, but her foot in its sandal was still whole, standing on the pedestal. Also new, since Ellen had last seen her, were the frilly scabs of yellow lichen that had once been no more than little freckles. One was starting to grow over her right eye, like a pirate's patch, but in spite of it she was smiling gently with that coy, sidelong look upwards.

The shell was full of dead leaves and seed heads, and Kasey stirred it with her finger. Woodlice and leggy spiders ran about.

"Poor thing. Fancy leaving her here." Kasey did not jump and scream at the spiders.

"She's broken," Ellen pointed out.

"Not much. I've seen more broken things than that in the museum; just feet sometimes. She might be hundreds of years old."

"I think she's a birdbath," Ellen said.

"So? I expect they had birdbaths hundreds of years ago," Kasey said. "She might be a goddess thingy."

"I thought she was, like, out of the church

when I first saw her," Ellen said. "I used to bow down to her."

"An idol."

"No, a saint. But she was bigger, then – I was smaller. I just thought it was polite. I was a bit scared of her."

"What, in case she came after you when you went through the fence and bit your bum?"

"*No.* But before the ivy grew so long she just used to stand there like that statue of the Virgin Mary outside the Catholic school in town."

"She's not the Virgin Mary, not showing all that leg," Kasey said, shrewdly. "How did you bow down? Go on, show us."

"Well … like this." Ellen dipped her head. "But at first I used to kneel down and say something."

"What? What did you say?"

"Nothing."

"Yes you did, you just told me. What did you say?"

"Well, I was *little* then – and you know what people say about going over the fields, how it's dangerous and that."

"Yes."

"I just used to say, 'Don't let anything bad happen to me.'" Ellen blushed at the memory.

"And did it?"

"What?"

"Did anything bad not happen to you?"

Ellen thought about it. "Yes ... I mean, no, nothing happened."

"Nobody jumped you, or nothing?"

"No, never."

"Did you ever ask her for anything else?"

"I never really *asked* her. In the end I just used to, like, touch her for good luck as I went by." And in the end she had not even done that. She could not remember when she had started to forget about the lady, and had rushed past her, going and coming, unheeding, unseeing, while the strangely scented ivy swarmed up the fence and fell back upon itself to shroud the lady in its mysterious leaves. "Well, I did sort of ask, when my granny was ill." She suddenly saw which way Kasey's thoughts were running. "It was only pretending, like a joke."

But Granny's illness had been no joke.

"Did she get better, your nan?"

"Yes. I mean, she wasn't *very* ill, well, she was, but I didn't know. She had an operation. I must have told you."

"Yes. It was years and years ago. Did you give her anything?"

"Who, Granny? Well, flowers, and I made her a card—"

"*No*, the lady with iron bones."

"What for give her things?"

"You ought to have. So she'd know you were grateful."

38

"But she didn't do anything."

Kasey was scraping out the dead leaves from the shell with her cupped hands, lifting them gently so as not to disturb the scrambling insects too much. With a flat leaf she patiently rounded up the last woodlice and deposited them by the fence where there was plenty of humus to hide in. The outside of the shell was ridged like a giant cockle, but inside it was a smooth shallow bowl, stained green in rings from pale lime at the top to deepest jade, where rainwater had collected and dried away. Ellen was sure it was meant to be a birdbath.

"You could put things in it now," Kasey said.

"What things?"

"Just things." She rearranged the ivy over the statue. "If that was mine I'd get her mended. I wouldn't hide her down here. You wanted to show me something. Was it her?"

Ellen, glad to be leaving the hazards of Mrs Sayer's garden, shifted the loose fence boards.

"This is how I go in and out."

"Go where?"

"Over the fields. To the Blasted Oak."

"What's that, then?"

"It's a tree that got struck by lightning. You must have seen it."

"I don't come here. Not allowed." Kasey tossed that in almost as a snub to her, Ellen thought. *My mum might have post-natal*

39

depression and her old man's run off but she doesn't let me go over the fields. There are limits. She followed Ellen through the loose boards and out on to the grass, where the jagged outline of the Blasted Oak reared up ahead of them on the mound formed by its own roots.

"Oh, that old thing," Kasey said. "Why d'you want to show me that?" She sounded disappointed, as if Ellen had oversold the Blasted Oak.

"It's my special place."

"It's only a dead tree."

"Yes, but look at this grass inside, it's all soft, like a cushion. When I sit in here, no one can see me."

"You just *sit* here?" Kasey's tone implied that she, personally, had no time for just sitting.

"I read, sometimes. And look, you can see where the wood got burnt when the lightning struck."

"It's like a tooth," Kasey said, sniffily. "Like one of those big ones at the back, gone rotten."

"We could both sit in it. There's room."

"Naaah." Kasey, restless and discontented, kicked at the tree roots and fiddled with her earrings. "It's boring. People don't even snog here. Let's go back."

They trailed down the mound and returned to the fence, Ellen first. She did not look round to see if Kasey were following, and was through the fence, under the hedge and back in her own garden before she realized that Kasey was no longer behind her. She turned and looked through the gap. Kasey was still by Mrs Sayer's fence, adjusting the ivy fronds.

"Come *on*," Ellen hissed. "You don't have to tidy up."

"Just saying goodbye to your Lady Ironbones," Kasey said.

They went back to the flat where Mum and Macauley were making towers with Ellen's old building bricks, Mum building the towers and Mac knocking them down with accurate swipes with the flat of his hand.

"That's right, smash everything up," Kasey said.

Ellen saw Mum frown, but she was smiling again when she looked up at Kasey.

"We're making progress. To start with he knocked them over as soon as I put one on top of the other. Now we're getting to five or six. They fall over on their own, after that. The carpet's bumpy. Do you want a drink?"

She got up and headed for the kitchen. Kasey hovered. "What about Mac?"

"I fenced him in," Mum said. Macauley was hedged around with a stockade formed by the settee, two chairs and a coffee table. He sat like a large toad, contemplating the bricks. Kasey followed Ellen into the kitchen.

"He could *climb* out – only he can't stand up," she conceded, as Mum took coffee mugs out of the drying rack and switched on the kettle. "I mean, he can stand up and if you hold his hands he can walk, well, not walk, but he puts one foot in front of the other. He's not backward or nothing, he just won't try." The corners of her mouth turned down. "Doesn't even crawl."

"Ellen never crawled at all," Mum said. "She just waited until she could walk, and then she walked."

"How old?" Kasey demanded, anxiously.

Ellen tried not to feel resentful, but it was hard when Mum said, "Oh, twenty months at least, I should think."

They were not discussing her, only the baby she had once been, that she could not even remember being, but when Kasey turned away for a moment she scowled at Mum to let her know what she was thinking. It had been a lot earlier than twenty months.

Mum caught her eye and made a face, woman to woman. *Give the girl a break. Can't you see she's worried? I know you could walk when you were one.*

"What's that thing?" Kasey said.

"A cafetière."

"Caffy – what you make coffee in? Does it boil itself? What's that bit for?"

Mum showed her how the cafetière worked.

42

Ellen looked in at the living room door. Macauley, left to himself, was placing a red brick with scientific precision on top of a blue one. Then he selected a yellow brick, moved the blue, replaced it with the yellow and balanced the blue on top of that.

"B'ick," he said, carefully. Then he noticed Ellen watching him and sent his tower flying with a petulant swat.

Oh, so that's your game, is it? Ellen thought. You know how Kasey worries about you and you're just winding her up. She was appalled that someone so small should be so cunning. She made sure that Mac saw her give a scornful shrug, and turned her back.

Kasey was standing by Mum, cooing over the cafetière. She turned quickly when she felt Ellen standing behind them.

"Is he all right – better check—"

"He's fine." Ellen decided not to tell Kasey about Mac's building operations. Let her find out for herself, it would be more fun.

They took the coffee into the living room where Macauley turned into a toad again, glaring at the bricks and banging his feeding bottle on them. Mum nodded towards the television.

"Has he got a favourite programme?"

"I don't like him watching too much telly," Kasey said. "It's all right now and again but if you let him he just sits there gawping at it all

43

day. It's bad for them, isn't it? Does their eyes in. I'm not being rude, or anything. We'll have it on if you want. It's your house."

Ellen realized that Kasey must like Mum a lot to worry about offending her.

"Whatever you think best," Mum said. She sat next to Kasey on the settee with Mac squatting at their feet. Ellen looked at them from time to time. There was something different about Kasey. She leaned back against the cushions, making herself at home, but after a few minutes her eye wandered to the clock and she became fidgety again.

"I'd better get back. Mum'll be worried. Thanks for the coffee. Thanks for looking after Mac."

Mum came down with them and helped Kasey to squeeze Macauley into his buggy and carry it down the steps to the gate, where they stood chatting like old friends over Mac's head. Ellen left them to it and went back upstairs to fetch the cafetière. Mum did not like flushing the grounds down the sink in case they clogged the drain, and she had some idea that they made good compost, so they were always scooped out and scattered around the roots of plants. When Ellen came out again Mum and Kasey were still talking. *Gossiping*, Ellen thought. Hard to believe that half an hour ago Kasey had been asking if the lady with iron bones was a goddess; which reminded her of something.

She sidled along the hedge to the end of the garden, ducked under the thorns and went straight to Mrs Sayer's back fence where the ivy swayed gently as she disturbed the air around it. She parted the fronds and looked into the dark cavern beyond. The lady with iron bones stood as she always did, head bent, smiling up from the shell in her hands, as if she had seen something nice or funny in it. After Kasey had cleaned out the leaves and insects the bowl had been empty, but now, at the bottom, lay a single rose, one of the peppermint-striped ones that grew on the bush by the rubbish heap. It could not have got there by accident. In that half-minute when Ellen had gone under the hedge and Kasey had waited behind, she must have darted to the bush, pulled off the flower and placed it in the bowl of the shell.

Whatever for ... out of pity? Kasey had been scandalized to think that anything as beautiful and mysterious as the lady with iron bones should be left forgotten and neglected behind the rubbish heap, even if her leg was falling off. Could the rose be meant to cheer her up?

Kasey had never gone in for let's pretend. Even when they were both little she had preferred ball games and skipping ropes and just running about, to being pop singers or princesses. Ellen recalled how she had stood here, asking all those questions about bowing down to the lady and praying to her. It had only been a game, Ellen thought. Not even a game, more like touching wood for good luck and believing it had worked because you got what you wanted, or blaming an accident on the fact that you had walked on a crack in the pavement.

She remembered, too, Kasey in assembly, Kasey in church, eyes shut, hands clenched; *Please. Please. Please. Please.* Kasey today, disappointed, resigned; *I knew it wouldn't work.* Had she given the lady with iron bones a rose because she had asked her for something? Had Kasey been praying to *her*? Was the rose an offering or simply a present? They were not the same thing.

She began to wish that she had not said anything about the lady's good-luck properties, but who could have imagined that Kasey would take it so seriously, take it seriously at all? Still, Kasey was getting desperate, ready to try anything although Kray had been gone scarcely four days. His disappearance was not the only thing she had to worry about, but it must be the last straw. What would she do when he failed to come back? Ellen knew that Kray hit out when he was in a temper, not at people but at things. She had once seen him punching the back of a bus. There were dents in the Carters' walls from Kray's knuckles, which often had a scabby look to them. She thought of Kasey venting her disappointment on the lady. It wouldn't take much to knock off a few more bits of concrete – her head for instance. Did she have an iron neck, too?

Distantly a door banged, not her own; it must be one of the Sayers going in or out. Ellen started to leap at the hedge, then hesitated, steeled herself and edged closer to the rubbish heap which was almost hidden now by the overhanging rose bush. She listened intently and heard heels clicking towards her over the pavement of the garden path. Someone was coming down the garden. If Kasey was right, whoever it was would not see Ellen before Ellen saw them. The footsteps came nearer, nearer, then a small shower of carrot scrapings and cabbage leaves descended on the rubbish heap. The footsteps receded.

Ellen craned her neck, but whoever had come down the garden, and was now going up it, had not seen her. They had stood on the path, aimed the kitchen scraps and gone away again.

Ellen crept over to the ivy, took one more look at the lady with her rose, and went back. As she walked down her own path she noticed that she was still carrying the cafetière.

"Where've you been?" Mum was rinsing out the coffee mugs.

"Just emptying this." Ellen handed her the glass jug as Mum's hand in its soapy rubber glove reached out for it. "She's all right, isn't she?" she went on, to change the subject, before Mum could ask her why it had taken ten minutes to empty the cafetière.

"Who?"

"Kasey."

"Yes. She's a lot brighter than I thought."

"*Mum.*"

"Well, I never thought she was stupid – but she's always so sulky, snappish."

"She just doesn't say much."

"It's not what she doesn't say, it's the way she doesn't say it. Still, she said plenty today. She worries a lot about that baby, doesn't she?"

"It's because…" Ellen hesitated. She did not want to sound like one of those mothers at the school gate. "You know … her mum. She doesn't look after him properly."

"It's not that she doesn't bother—"

"But she doesn't, does she?" Ellen said. "She's in bed half the time."

"So would you be if you were ill."

"She's not ill, she's depressed. Everyone knows."

"Everyone doesn't know. If they did they might be more sympathetic. Depression's an illness. She was fine before Mac came along; don't you remember?"

Ellen tried to think back to eighteen months ago, but that was when Granny had been so ill. It was hard to remember anything else clearly, even Emily gleefully informing them all that Kasey Carter's dad had walked out.

"But Kasey's always been like – like she is," Ellen said. "*She's* not depressed or anything."

"That's just Kasey, isn't it? Her way of coping, and she's got enough to cope with. It might be an idea if you brought her round here more often."

"Why?"

"Don't you want to?"

"Yes – but she thinks you don't like her."

Mum looked thoughtful, almost ashamed. "I've never been unkind to her, have I? I've hardly ever had the chance to speak to her."

"She just knew," Ellen said. "Anyway, she likes you."

"We'll see if we can't get Mac up and running. That might cheer everyone up a bit. It must be like having a live suet pudding in the house with him around."

"I thought he was like a toad," Ellen said.

"It's the way he sits. You expect a long tongue to shoot out and scoop flies off the wall."

"He puts it on," Ellen said. "When you were making coffee with Kasey, I watched him. He was building towers with those bricks. And he said 'brick'. Well, almost."

"He's a little brute," Mum said, in the same voice she might have used to say, "He's a little angel."

CHAPTER FOUR

It had been Zara Fisher who first took the lady with iron bones seriously.

Ellen had forgotten Zara Fisher. When Mum and Ellen first moved into their flat, the Fishers had lived in the one downstairs. Zara had been in the year below Ellen so she was not someone Ellen had to bother about at school. She was one of the girls who sat on the low wall outside the staffroom at break, and shared little glittery things that they kept in furry purses or sequined handbags. There was something hopelessly frilly about Zara: ruffles round her socks, bows on her skirts, pink hearts embroidered on her jeans. Even her T-shirts had lace on.

Before the Walcotts put up their hostile larch-lap, the back garden of the downstairs flat had been fenced off with rickety chestnut palings, through which Zara and her even frillier little sister could be seen hostessing Barbie tea parties. But one day Ellen encountered Zara in the gap under the hedge as she was going out of Mrs Sayer's garden and Zara was coming in. Ellen was crawling, Zara approaching from the other direction in a mincing duckwalk so as not to soil the knees of her pink and blue leggings or the toes of her white trainers. They were the three-storey kind with windows in the ground floor, and at the end of her spindly legs made her look like a carthorse colt.

"What are you doing here?" Zara said, as they stalled in the tunnel.

"What are *you* doing here?"

"I asked first."

"I was here first."

"Where?"

"This is *my* end of the garden, this bit. That's yours." Ellen pointed to the chestnut palings. Zara was committing a double trespass.

"I'm exploring," Zara said. "Like on television." Only someone as dimly damp as Zara would need to find out about exploring from something she had seen on television, as if it never happened in real life. "Anyway, I *lived* here first."

Just listening to Zara's gnat-like whine made Ellen want to push her over and jump up and down on her head. "You're trespassing, not exploring," Ellen said.

"So are you."

"No I'm not."

"You are if you don't live here."

"I do live here, and this is my garden, not yours."

"You don't live on *this* side."

"Nor do you."

"That's different," Zara chanted triumphantly. "Mrs Sayer is our friend."

Ellen could not say the same thing. Mum and Mrs Sayer were polite to each other when they met, but they did not meet often. Mrs Sayer was not young and rarely went out except, so far as Ellen knew, down to her rubbish heap. Sometimes there was someone else in the garden, another woman, who did not seem to be quite so old, and once or twice Ellen caught sight of a man, digging or mowing the lawn. Mum and Mrs Sayer occasionally took in parcels for one another but otherwise they did not run into each other by chance. When a hearse pulled up outside one day and a coffin came out, Ellen had been astounded to hear Mum say, "Old Mr Sayer's died." She had not even known that there was a Mr Sayer. Mum sent something that she said was a letter of condolence.

Mrs Sayer did not know that Ellen used her garden as a short cut to the fields.

"It's ever so wet," Zara was complaining, as

they elbowed each other out into Mrs Sayer's property.

"That's because the sun doesn't shine on this bit."

"And why—" Zara caught sight of the lady with iron bones. "Oh, isn't she creepy?"

"No she's not." In fact the lady with iron bones had been looking downright skittish that day. At the weekend Ellen had made a daisy chain over in the fields and on the way home had tossed it over the lady's head where it hung like a necklace. She did things like that to test Mrs Sayer, in the hope that Mrs Sayer would think the end of her garden was haunted. That Mrs Sayer might come up with quite a different explanation did not occur to her then.

"Who put those flowers round her?" Zara squeaked.

"I dunno. Maybe she went and picked them herself. Maybe it was fairies."

This was meant to be the cue for Zara to turn in a huff and go back under the hedge, taking her Barbie handbag with her, but it backfired. Zara put her head on one side and a half-witted smile spread across her face.

"Oh! Is she the fairy queen?"

"Haven't you seen her before? I thought you said Mrs Sayer was your friend."

"She *is*. We had tea on her *patio*!" Zara nodded towards the strip of paving under Mrs

Sayer's back windows. "But we didn't come down this mucky old bit. I only came just now to see where you were going."

"Well, now you know. Why don't you go home?" Ellen said, but Zara was whining on, "I saw a fairy once."

"Where, at the bottom of the dustbin?"

"No, really, it was real, well, I think it was, I *think* I saw it. You know, off to one side, when you see something you're not looking at."

Ellen did know, but was in no mood to encourage Zara.

"Naaah."

"Well, I did. I made a wish, and I left out some bubble gum on a leaf."

"For the fairy?" What kind of a fairy chewed gum? Some sort of heavy-metal elf, perhaps, in black leather and DMs, blowing pink bubbles. "Did it come true, your wish?"

Zara went all round-eyed and mystic. "I wished for a Barbie kitchen for Christmas, and I got it."

"I expect you'd have got it anyway," Ellen said, cruelly. Most of Zara's possessions involved Barbie in some shape or form. She suddenly realized who Zara reminded her of.

Zara was being called from her back door. "I'll see you soon," she promised and disappeared under the hedge.

"Not if I can help it," Ellen muttered

to herself.

Two days later, on her way to the Blasted Oak, where Zara was never allowed to go, she saw that in place of the withered daisy chain the lady with iron bones was wearing a necklace of Christmas-tree baubles strung on moulting tinsel. Ellen ripped it off and was about to chuck it over the hedge when she had a better idea and shoved it in her pocket. Next morning Zara sidled up to her in the playground.

"You know the fairy queen?"

"Go away – *infant*," Ellen said, although Zara was in Year 3. Zara could not take a hint and continued to hover.

"I made her a necklace and it's disappeared, like the bubble gum."

"What *is* she on about?" Kasey said.

"Oh, just some baby game she's playing. She thinks she found a fairy."

"I wished my auntie would come to stay and she's stopping the night on Saturday," Zara persisted. "She's taking me shopping."

Kasey turned round and growled which was all it took to send Zara scuttling back to her friends on the wall outside the staffroom.

Fortunately Zara grew careless and soon her mother noticed that the triple-decker trainers were coming in covered in mud, and Zara was forbidden to make any more visits under the hedge. Occasionally at school she would appear at Ellen's elbow, whingeing, "Make a wish for me, Ellen. Give her this," and some shining object would be pressed into her hand to pass on to the lady with iron bones, but after a while she seemed to forget about her and soon after that the Fishers moved out, the Walcotts moved in, and the larch-lap fence went up.

Ellen had never told Zara that she herself used the lady with iron bones as a good-luck charm. It was only when she saw the red and white rose in the shell that she remembered Zara and her fairies. Had Kasey remembered too? No, Kasey had never known what Zara was rabbiting on about.

What ought she to do? Take the rose and let Kasey think that the lady had somehow absorbed it – as the fairy had eaten the bubble gum? What did Kasey expect to happen? Somewhere in Ellen's wardrobe were the bauble necklace, bits of glitter and Christmas-cracker trinkets that Zara had given her to give to the lady with iron bones. Ellen had felt guilty about them ever since, but could not bring herself to throw them out. She had wondered about giving them back to Zara, until Zara had moved away and the problem had solved itself, but her conscience still gnawed her. She had not taken the things for Zara's sake, to keep up the make-believe, but only because they infuriated her and Zara infuriated her. Surely she had not really believed in fairies, even gum-chewing ones, any more than Kasey could believe that the lady would come down off her pedestal at night and take her rose to some secret stash – but what did Kasey believe? God had failed her. Was she really pinning her faith on a bird-bath?

"Last in, first out," Mrs Bean said to Kasey on Monday, knowing that come half past three Kasey would be out of the door faster than a greased weasel. Kasey was third on the register and Mrs Bean had reached William Young-man, who was at the end of it.

On Tuesday she cut it even finer; they were lining up for assembly; but on Wednesday Kasey was on time; only just, she was the last in, but the second bell was still ringing. She did not even glance at Mrs Bean's surprised face but walked straight to the table and sat down next to Ellen. She was not smiling but Ellen could see that she was trying not to, instead of letting her mouth droop into the weary lines that it usually did. Her face actually looked rounder, her eyes wider, perhaps because her eyebrows were not drawn towards her nose.

"What's happened?" Ellen mouthed.

While the register was called, they were supposed to sit down without talking or fidgeting. Ellen had her back to Mrs Bean.

Kasey was facing her, but even so she risked saying, "He's phoned."

"Kasey!" Mrs Bean's laser eyes were roving over the class, even though she seemed to be looking at the register.

"Kray?"

Ellen had not made a sound but Mrs Bean said, "What did you say, Ellen?"

"Nothing, Miss."

Under cover of this exchange Kasey hissed, "Yes," and got away with it.

Mrs Bean was on full beam now. Ellen dared not ask any more questions and knew she would have to wait right through assembly before she could pump Kasey for details, and Kasey, for once, looked as if she was dying to tell. On television people told each other things in church by pretending to sing hymns and putting other words to them, but she did not think Mrs Bean would fail to spot her singing, "When did Kray ring up?" instead of "Kumbaya, My Lord, Kumbaya". Mrs Bean could lip-read, they all knew that.

Assembly took longer than usual because the head teacher had notices to read out about Sports Day and the end-of-term fête.

"Anyone who can bring food for the produce stall see Miss Beckett in the Year 2 mobile," Mr Lewis said. "Miss Hoskins in Year 5 is arranging the plant stall so go and see her if you can bring anything – but no plants yet – or food, come to think of it. There's over three weeks to go. But you can take second-hand clothes to Mrs Booker in Year 4 and bric-à-brac to Mrs Bean in Year 6, for the White Elephant stall. That includes books, tapes, videos and CDs. Got it?"

Then he said it all again because he knew that half of them had not got it. He even explained about white elephants this time round, and the Reception Class looked more confused than ever.

Ellen did not hear a word. She was conscious of Kasey beside her, almost fizzing, her lank hair seeming to rise up at the ends in electric waves of excitement, but they were back in the classroom before Kasey could say, "He rang up last night. I was just going to bed."

One of the reasons Kasey arrived late at school was that she seldom got to bed before midnight, sitting up to keep her sad mum company in the long evenings.

"What did he say?"

"He found his dad."

"How?"

"He just went round all the pubs, asking, one after the other. Never thought he'd have the sense."

"Is he a boozer, then, his dad?"

"Naaah. He's not an alkie or anything, but men go to pubs, don't they. I mean, when they haven't got anything else to do or nowhere to go, they go down the pub." Ellen deferred to Kasey's wider knowledge of what men did. She had little to go on. There was no man at home; there never had been. "Well, Kray went into every pub and asked if anyone knew Kevin Robson, 'cause he guessed he'd have a local."

"He might have changed his name."

"Why should he? He isn't on the run."

"But there must be hundreds of pubs in Birmingham."

"There are," Kasey said, "but he had a plan." She sounded awestruck at the thought and Ellen, knowing Kray, could understand why. "He knew his dad would never go any-where with a stupid name like, oh, the Bog and Barmaid, nothing like that, so he got a Yellow Pages, and tore the pub bits out and went through them. And I'll tell you what, he didn't think of that at first. He didn't think of it till Sunday evening."

"So?" That made it four days; much more Kray's speed.

"That was when I asked your lady."

"You what?"

"When I came round yours and you took me to see the Blasted Oak while your mum looked after Mac and we found the lady with iron bones."

"You found her," Ellen said. She had an unwelcome preview of what was coming. "I knew she was there."

All around them people were settling at their tables, taking out files and books, spilling pens and crayons. At the teacher's desk Mrs Bean was working herself up to demand that people got down to their English work. With her folder, Ellen managed to send the pot of pens on their table tottering, and as they scattered over the floor Kasey dived down with her to help gather them up.

"You never thought she could do anything?"

"Why not? I gave her a rose and asked."

"What did you say?"

"Same as I did to—" Kasey shrugged scornfully ceiling-ward. Ellen, who did not actually believe in God, suddenly found herself hoping he was not listening. "Only *she* noticed. *She* did something."

"Kasey, she's a birdbath. She's made of concrete."

"So's that old Virgin Mary outside the Catholic school. And what about all those Jesuses hanging up? Plaster."

Ellen noticed that among the chair legs and table legs were now two human ones. Staring up at Mrs Bean must be like standing at the foot of the Statue of Liberty.

"Have you *quite* finished?" Mrs Bean said.

Ellen reached out for a last fugitive pencil and rammed it into the pot. She and Kasey stood up together.

"If this is how you're going to behave perhaps you had better go back to being late again," Mrs Bean said to Kasey, although it was Ellen who had upset the pencil pot. "No, forget I said that," she added, as the mutinous scowl began to form pleats in Kasey's forehead, as if someone had pulled a thread and drawn her skin together. She sat down with a wallop, like a dropped backpack, and guided her book towards her with her elbow, turning it right way round with a series of jabs.

Ellen would have to wait for break before she found out the rest, although she was not at all sure that she wanted to hear the rest. Kasey, solemn, sullen Kasey, really believed that the lady with iron bones had heard her prayer and granted it, in return for a rose.

"I'll have to give her something," Kasey said, at break.

"You already did. You gave her the rose."

"That's not the same. It was just like being polite, like saying 'Please Miss', before you talk. So people know you're going to talk. So they'll listen."

"To make sure she took notice?"

"Sort of. So she knew I meant it."

"Well, she does know. You don't have to—" Ellen wanted to say, "You don't have to make a habit of it."

"I *do*. I haven't told you everything. Kray

says he'll be home at the weekend. He promised."

"And you think if you don't give the lady another present she'll change her mind and he'll stay in Birmingham?"

"I got to say thank you, haven't I?" The scowl that was never far away began to gather between her eyebrows. "I mean if you gave me something and I never said thank you, you wouldn't give me anything else, probably. You might take it away again."

"I *wouldn't.*"

"Well, you aren't her, are you? Look, can I come round yours after school?"

"What for?" Ellen said, knowing quite well. "Won't your mum worry?" she added, craftily.

"Not for *long,*" Kasey said. "You weren't bothered about me being late when you got me up the church, were you?"

Ellen wished that she had never suggested to Kasey that they went to the church. It was the sight of Kasey praying in assembly that had done it. She ought not to have encouraged Kasey to do what she would not do herself, to believe in something that she did not believe. But wishing was no use. It was done. It could not be undone.

"Do you want a drink or something?" Ellen asked as they walked up the path, and half drew the key from the neck of her shirt. At the back of her mind was the idea of delaying tactics, keeping Kasey amused with food, drink, television – anything – until she realized how late it was and fled home without having had time to visit the lady with iron bones.

Kasey was not to be diverted. "I haven't got long. You needn't come if you don't want to."

Ellen followed her round the side of the house, past the back door and along the hedge. Mrs Sayer's garden seemed deserted as usual, doors shut, sash windows down. She felt faintly put out; who did Kasey think she was, to lead the way in *her* garden, to go first under the hedge, *her* hedge?

Kasey was down on her knees before she stopped, looked up and said, "You don't have to come too."

"It's all right," Ellen said, starting to stoop, then she saw by Kasey's look that Kasey had meant, "I don't *want* you to come too." She stood up again and watched Kasey's trainers disappear among the grasses. She did not follow but tried to see through the foliage. Serve Kasey right if Mrs Sayer, in rubber heels for once, came pussy-footing down her garden path and caught Kasey mucking around with her birdbath. She thought she heard voices. She did hear voices, one voice, Kasey, talking to herself; talking to the lady with iron bones.

After a minute or two Kasey re-emerged.

Ellen felt like saying sarcastically, "Had a good natter, then?" but sarcasm was a dangerous weapon with Kasey. It might wound, but equally it might bounce back and hit the hitter.

"Better get back," Kasey said, before Ellen could speak. "See you tomorrow, eh?"

"You going to be on time again and give Old Mother Bean a heart attack?" Ellen called after her, finally thinking of something to say.

"That's right." Kasey was almost running, but she turned, without stopping, to answer Ellen, then turned again so that she seemed to be skipping, or dancing.

Ellen stood, listening to her footsteps echo between the two houses and thud down the front path. The gate snecked. Kasey was gone. Ellen went down on hands and knees and crawled under the hedge. The end of the garden looked as it always did, but the curtain of ivy was still swaying gently. Ellen went over and drew it to one side. The lady looked up at her coyly, askance, holding out the shell. *Look what I've got.*

Where the rose had been – Kasey must have tossed it aside – lay something shining in the jade-green bowl; two things. Ellen touched them, then picked them up. She knew at once what they were, had seen them often enough; every day nearly. Kasey had given her earrings to the lady with iron bones.

CHAPTER FIVE

Here was something else to wish she had not done. There had been no need to go snooping in Mrs Sayer's garden to see what Kasey had been up to.

The earrings were probably the most valuable things that Kasey owned, which must be what had made her give them to the lady. She loved them and, not allowed to wear them in school, put them on the moment she was out of the gate. They could not be worth all that much really, but it seemed ridiculous to leave them out here in the garden. What did Kasey imagine the lady with iron bones would do with them; wear them? On the other hand, if she took them away Kasey might go back to look and wonder where they had gone; demand to know where they had gone, and if it had been Ellen who had taken them, Kasey would know. She could always tell what Ellen was thinking – and anyone else, come to that. It must be the result of having to stay one jump ahead of her mother, having to know how she felt before it was too late to do anything about it.

The earrings sparkled like little chandeliers. Ellen twirled the posts in her fingers to make them catch the light, then laid them back down in the bowl of the birdbath. If Kasey really imagined that the lady with iron bones was somehow going to come to life and take the earrings she would just have to deal with the disappointment. As she went back under the hedge she thought of drippy Zara and how she had taken the baubles that Zara had left for her fairy queen, and the other things that Zara had trusted her with afterwards. Kasey was not Zara. She was used to disappointment. Ellen was not going to start that nonsense all over again.

In the end she left the earrings in the bowl and found a fallen leaf to cover them with. The lady was well sheltered but it seemed careless to leave them exposed. No one else would come looking but there were magpies in the trees over in the fields. Ellen had heard that magpies liked shiny things and stole jewellery, although she could not imagine what they did with it. Gave it to lady magpies, perhaps.

Mum came home at five on the dot, just as Ellen switched the kettle on.

"You'll never guess who I just met," she said, pushing her bike into its summer parking bay behind the wheelie bin as Ellen opened the door.

"Who?" Ellen said, not even trying to guess. It might well be someone she had never heard of.

"Lyndsay Carter, in the Co-op."

Ellen had to think for a moment before she remembered who Lyndsay Carter was.

"Kasey's mum?"

"Yes. She was buying bread."

"What did she say?"

"Didn't say anything to me. She was at the checkout as I went in. But it's the first time I've seen her out in months."

"Was Kasey with her?"

"No, only Macauley – bring the shopping in, will you? I didn't see Kasey. Why, wasn't she at school again?"

"Yes, she was." Ellen said no more. She did not want to get to a point in a conversation with Mum where she would have to explain about Kray coming home. She did not know if Mum knew about Kray going away, and why he had done it. Mum was no gossip but she must pick things up from people at work or places like the Co-op, in which case what she had picked up might well be wide of the mark. Mum hardly knew Mrs Carter, but she was sympathetic, which was more than a lot of people were, the grown-up versions of Emily: *Look at those kids … that boy's never had a job in his life … Kasey? Something wrong there…*

To change the subject she said, "Our class is doing the White Elephant stall at the fête. Have we got anything I could take? Videos would do."

"I bet they would," Mum said. She sat on the kitchen table looking through the letters that had arrived after she left for work, nibbling a biscuit and waiting for the tea to brew. Ellen went into the living room and switched the television on, seeing faces, hearing voices, without looking at them or listening to them. She thought of the earrings. Kasey had given them to the lady with iron bones in return for Kray's phone call and his promise to return home. Then, presumably, she had gone home herself to find that her mother was shopping with Mac. Would Kasey decide that she had to thank the lady for that, too? What was she planning to give her next?

There were two days to the weekend, one and a bit if you counted Friday night as the beginning of it. And four days till it ended. She could not start to imagine how Kasey was going to be feeling during those three days till she could expect her brother to walk in; how she would feel during the next two, waiting for his key in the lock every second; how she would feel on Sunday night if he had not come home after all. Ellen could not bear even to think about that. She had nothing to compare it with. She could not ever remember wanting anything so much, and Kasey, of course, did not even want it for herself. It was her mum who needed Kray to come back.

At least Kasey wasn't asking for her own dad back; that really would have been asking for trouble, absolute guarantee of failure. Ellen had no experience of that kind of disappointment. She had never known a dad to lose and find again, she had been too young to be really worried when Granny was ill, only miserable and uneasy because Mum was so upset. If Granny had died she would not have been disappointed, only terribly sad because she would never see her again. But she did not see Granny all that often anyway ... not even *terribly* sad. It was so long ago. Had she understood then how it would feel to lose someone you really cared about? Would she understand now?

"Are you watching this rubbish?" Mum said, looking in on her way to the computer.

Ellen jumped guiltily. "No – yes – sort of—"

"I don't mind," Mum said, "but if you're not watching, turn it off. Turn it down, anyway. You're sitting on the remote."

She went out again. The television was really blaring now, some team game involving green slime, a sandpit and giant inflatable frogs. Ellen zapped it with the remote and the sound dwindled.

What *would* Kasey do if Kray did not come home at the weekend?

Mum gave her a carrier bag of skirts and sweaters for the fête and three videos that they decided they could live without. On Thursday morning Ellen took the carrier to Mrs Booker in the next room before giving Mrs Bean the videos.

"In the stockroom," Mrs Bean said. "I've started a box. There's a picture of a white elephant on it, for people who can't read."

The box was a big deep one, by the door, and there were already things in it. Ellen was just starting to poke about among them when she saw Kasey stalking by, leisurely, not even one of the last in.

"What you doing in there?" Kasey said, noticing Ellen in the doorway.

"Stuff for the fête." Ellen came out quickly before Mrs Bean could pounce on Kasey for going into the stockroom without permission, but Kasey was already passing the teacher's desk.

"Morning Mrs Bean," she said, giving Mrs Bean no chance to say anything, and swerved away towards her table.

"You been down to see the lady?" she said,

when Ellen caught up.

"No," Ellen said, as casually as Kasey had said, "Morning Mrs Bean". She was opening her book bag at the time and did not have to look at Kasey when she answered. "Why?"

"Just *asked*," Kasey said aggressively, to Ellen's relief. Kasey was satisfied and Ellen would not have to ask any more questions although she said "Sorry", to be on the safe side. She knew why Kasey had asked *her* question. Now that she had lied about the reason for asking, the boundaries were drawn. It was official; Ellen did not know what Kasey had given to the lady with iron bones.

At break, though, she had to say *something*.

"My mum saw your mum in the Co-op yesterday."

Kasey almost glowed. If anyone else had said that she would have snarled, "Want to make something of it?" but now she simply said, "Yes, when I got home she'd taken Mac. She left a note."

Ellen thought of Granny's operation. Mum had come back from the hospital smiling, for the first time in ages. "She walked round the bed. I saw her."

Ellen, at the time, had felt faintly confused. She had had a picture of a big hospital ward, like on television, with beds down both sides, and curtains, and Granny's bed out in the middle of the floor, and Granny walking in circles, round and round it. Now she knew what a triumph it had been and understood how Kasey was feeling because her mum had gone down to the Co-op and bought a loaf of bread.

And yet, there were dark alleys down which Kasey's thoughts and feelings wandered where Ellen could not follow. Kasey thought that it was the lady with iron bones who had made Granny recover, who was snatching Kray from the jaws of Birmingham, who had made her mother feel well enough to go shopping.

Oh, make Kray come back like he said, she thought, and stopped. Who was she asking?

"Wassamatter?" Kasey was walking ahead and turned sharply when she noticed that Ellen had fallen behind.

"Something in my trainer," Ellen said, giving herself the excuse to untie it, shake out the imaginary foreign body and put it on again. At the back of her mind was the image of a telephone. Kray had been gone nearly a week. It would not have killed him to ring his mum sooner, to let her know that he was all right, before he found his dad. He might be lying about coming home.

Kasey might be thinking the same thing.

It was only as they left the playground at the end of the afternoon that she realized how complicated things were becoming. Usually, as they reached the gate, Kasey dug out her earrings and hooked them in. Of course she could not do it today, the earrings were in the lady's seashell, but Ellen was not supposed to know that. If she said anything, Kasey might turn suspicious. Ellen was not sure if she could say it naturally, but then she saw Kasey's hand go automatically to her pocket, fumble, come away empty.

"You haven't lost them, have you?"

"Lost what?"

"Your earrings."

"What's it to you?"

"Well, you always keep them in your pocket."

She saw Kasey relax. "Oh, I forgot. I didn't bring them today."

Kasey scraped back her hair and Ellen saw that she was wearing plain studs in her ears, the kind that are put in when they are first pierced. "I was afraid I'd lose them," Kasey went on, unnecessarily. She was beginning to gabble, the way people do who are making it up as they go along. "I mean, Kray gave them to me. I mean, I don't want to lose them just when he comes back. They fell out my pocket the other day and I only spotted them just in time. Someone else might have seen them and nicked them or they might have got trodden into the mud—"

"And no one would have found them for ages," Ellen chipped in, to help her out, "and then in a thousand years someone might come along with a metal detector—"

"And put them in a museum," Kasey said, "'cause they're *ever* so valuable—"

"Won't you ever wear them again?" Ellen asked, casually. This was Kasey's cue to confess, but she did not take it.

"I dunno," Kasey said. She fingered the studs. "These are better for school."

All the while they were walking down the hill, Ellen was expecting Kasey to suggest another visit to Mrs Sayer's garden, but when they reached the gate Kasey said, "See you tomorrow, then," and went on down the hill to the junction with Water Lane. Ellen walked up the steps and was about to open the side door when a thought struck her. She ran down the path to the end of the garden and slipped under the hedge, and without pausing to see if the coast was clear went to look in the lady's seashell. If Kasey was going to start lying to her, she could take what was coming. The lady would take the earrings. After all, that was what she was meant to do. If Kasey was going to act like Zara Fisher, serve her right.

She went straight to the fence, lifted the ivy and put her hand in the bowl, her fingertips encountering the dead leaf that she had left there herself.

But there was nothing under it. The lady *had* taken the earrings.

*　　*　　*

While Mum was watching the news on Channel 4 that evening Ellen went to her own room and burrowed at the bottom of the wardrobe among the dolls and teddies that she no longer played with but would never give away. In a crumpled paper bag, stuffed into her old nightdress case, she felt small round hard things: the necklace of Christmas baubles that Zara had made for the lady with iron bones.

Ellen took out the bag. It had been disturbed and squashed so many times that it felt almost like cloth. She unscrewed it and looked inside. The baubles were still shiny but the tinsel had gone yellow. Matted up with it were a pink plastic butterfly, a fancy button that looked pearly, a Barbie tiara, a ribbon bow off a gift box and a fridge magnet with a picture of Princess Diana on it.

Was this all? Ellen's conscience had persuaded her that Zara had given her dozens of things for the lady with iron bones. She crunched up the whole lot together in the bag. It could go in the kitchen swing bin. They were having pizza for supper. Mum would put the box on top of the bag and tomorrow the bin men would be along to take it all away.

As she stood up she looked out of the window. The room was so small that she could not help it, but as she turned away she saw someone crossing the fields towards the

Blasted Oak. Only adults used the footpath, cutting through to The Estate, or teenagers off for a snog beyond the rugby pitch, out of sight of the houses. This was neither teenager nor adult, but someone her own size, coming along at a trot, dodging from tree to tree as if afraid of being seen. People who moved like that usually looked over their shoulders to check if they were being followed. This person was looking one way all the time, straight at Ellen's flat, at her window. It was Kasey.

Ellen's first thought was to go to the window and wave, but knowing that Kasey had not seen her she drew back against the wall. It always seemed strange to her that although the white-painted room looked so bright when she was in it, it seemed dark and shadowy from out of doors, especially if it was sunny, as it was now. Kasey did not look as if she wanted to be seen and waved to. At any other time Ellen would have assumed that Kasey was coming to visit *her*, but now she did not think so, not at this time of the evening.

As if to prove her wrong Kasey instantly veered off the footpath, heading towards the end of the garden – no; to the end of Mrs Sayer's garden. Surely Kasey was not going to come through the gap in the fence, under the hedge, and sneak in to visit Ellen the back way? Suppose Mum looked out of *her* window and saw Kasey boldly strolling up the garden path? Officially she did not even know that Ellen went out that way, although Ellen was aware that she did know, and disapproved slightly, but not enough to go to the trouble of forbidding her to do it and then having to make sure that Ellen obeyed.

But even while she was thinking this, and wondering why Kasey had not yet emerged through the hedge, she knew the truth. Kasey was not coming to see her, she was coming to see the lady with iron bones.

Ellen sat down on the bed. If she had let Kasey know that she had been seen, would Kasey have pretended it was an ordinary visit? She had half a mind to go down now, creep under the hedge, and catch Kasey at whatever it was Kasey was doing, to make her jump guiltily when she was caught. Instead she kneeled on the bed, leaning against the wall, with her head against the curtain, eyes just above the level of the sill. The apple tree that concealed the end of Mrs Sayer's garden from the eyes of Mrs Sayer, also hid it from Ellen, but as soon as she saw Kasey returning on the footpath she would go down and find out what she had been up to.

She sat for ten minutes, and still Kasey did not emerge. Whatever she was doing, it had to have something to do with the earrings, for Kasey must be quite as surprised as Ellen to discover that they had gone. Or would she be?

Had she expected all along that the lady would accept her offering? Then Ellen heard someone ringing the doorbell, Mum going down to answer it and calling up the stairs, "Ellen! It's Kasey!"

They passed each other on the stairs.

"What's she want?" Ellen said.

Mum raised her eyebrows. "I don't know. She wouldn't come in."

Ellen was as shocked by her cunning as she had been by Mac's. It must run in the family. Kasey was covering her tracks. She had crept along the back fence to the footpath and come round to Ellen's door in case Ellen had seen her in the fields and wondered what she was doing. Should she tell Kasey that she *had* seen her and then ask where she had been for the last ten minutes, and what she had been doing, or wait until she went away again before going to find out?

Kasey stood in the little lobby at the foot of the stairs.

"I was just passing," she said, too offhandedly. "Thought I'd say hullo."

"Hullo," Ellen said unhelpfully.

"You know that book Mrs B said we ought to read?"

"Yes."

"I can't remember what it was called."

"Neither can I," Ellen said. Then she added, evilly, "You want to go and see the lady with

79

iron bones?"

"Oh no," Kasey said. "Not now. Got to get back." She turned to leave, then burst out, "You sure that next-door woman never goes down the end of her garden?"

Kasey was getting cold feet. Ellen said, "I've never seen her down there. Not past the rubbish heap."

"Oh well. Just thought I'd ask about the book. See you tomorrow, then."

"What was all that about?" Mum asked from the top of the stairs, as the door closed behind Kasey. "Why didn't you ask her in?"

"Oh, it was just something about school," Ellen said.

"Are you coming up?"

"In a minute."

"Supper's in ten," Mum said. She did not ask where Ellen was going. Occasionally Ellen realized just how much Mum could interfere if she felt like it, and was grateful for Mum's favourite motto: Life's too short. Still, she was glad that the kitchen window was at the front, so there was no one to see her on her way down the garden and under the hedge.

She could not help noticing that in only a few days the grass was getting a flattened look, not the smoothness of Mrs Sayer's lawn, but trampled and squashed. There was a permanent dent under the hedge, of course, but Ellen had always taken care never to let a path develop between the hedge and the fence. She saw no path now, but the grass and weeds around the place where the ivy hung down were bruised and crushed. It was all very well Kasey behaving like some secret agent out on the footpath, but that was no good if she was going to stomp around like a hippopotamus where somebody really might notice. Ellen stooped and stirred up the chickweed, brushing the grass erect again, bending stems back into position.

Then she remembered why she had come. Being careful where she put her feet she drew back the ivy curtains. Even in the greenish gloom she could see into the shell. For a moment she thought that she was looking at the leaf that had once concealed the earrings, but when she touched it she knew that this was something else, something flat and dark, soft, but hard under the softness.

Ellen stepped right under the ivy, next to the lady, and scooped it out. It was a red velvet slipcase with a mirror in it, a little circular handbag mirror with a gold backing that had a pattern of leaves stamped on it. Like the earrings it was probably not as expensive as it looked, but even so, it was not rubbish, not the kind of thing you could buy in the market, nor the kind of junk she had just tossed into the bin.

Ellen turned it over, not even seeing her own

face in it. Where had Kasey got this from? She did not own a handbag. Could she have nicked it from her mum? There was something familiar about it.

Ellen parted the curtains a little and looked harder. The case was not real velvet any more than the backing was real gold, but it looked brand new, not rubbed or scuffed. There were no specks on the glass. Surely Kasey had not stolen it from a shop?

She felt guilty even thinking it. Kasey had less money than anyone she knew, but she never stole things. She had too much respect for her own few possessions to take what belonged to other people. Once, not long ago, Kasey had found a pound coin in the grass while they were walking round the field at lunch time. "Keep it," Ellen had said. "I would." A pound was not to be sneezed at. "It's probably been there for weeks ... months." They had looked at the date, 1984, before they were born, even. "It could have been there for years."

"No, better hand it in," Kasey had said. "Someone might be looking for it. I mean, if *I'd* lost a pound I'd be out of my head."

She could never have stolen the handbag mirror; not even to give to the lady with iron bones. Ellen slipped it back into its case and laid it in the bowl of the shell. There was no need to cover this with a leaf ... where *had* the earrings gone? Maybe it was magpies after all.

If only she could ask, but she was not supposed to know about the earrings. She was certainly not supposed to know about the mirror which Kasey had put there only minutes ago. It was still a whole day yet till Friday night and the beginning of the weekend. Kasey was taking no chances.

CHAPTER SIX

On Friday morning the mirror was still lying in the birdbath. After school Kasey walked home with Ellen, urging her down the hill as if they were late for an appointment. When they reached Ellen's gate Kasey said abruptly, "You been down to see our lady?"

"No," Ellen said, equally abruptly, having no time to work out whether she would be telling the truth or lying.

"Let's go and see her now."

Maybe Ellen had said the right thing. If she was not supposed to know about the handbag mirror she would not have to act surprised if it had disappeared or act surprised if it was still there, but she did not much want to find out if it was there or not. She wished she had never found it, never found the earrings, never let Kasey find the lady with iron bones in the first place.

"Haven't you got to get home?" she said.

"No. Mum said she was going up the town this afternoon," and uninvited, Kasey pushed open Ellen's gate. "*Your* mum in?"

"She doesn't get home till five."

"Oh no, so she doesn't." Kasey looked genuinely sorry. "She's nice, your mum."

"I know." Once again Ellen found herself following Kasey up the steps and round the side of the house. When they reached the end of the hedge Ellen hung back, hoping Kasey would tell her to wait in her own garden as she had done last time they were here together, but Kasey said, "Come on," and dived out of sight.

"*Be careful*," Ellen said. One of these days Kasey was going to come face to face with Mrs Sayer making a surprise visit to her rubbish heap. She almost added a warning about the telltale signs that Kasey had left, the trodden weeds and bent grass stems, but remembered in time that this was something else she was not supposed to have seen.

Kasey was already at the ivy, parting the fronds and peering through. What does she expect to see? Ellen wondered. Or what does she expect not to see?

Kasey remained where she was, her head hidden by the ivy. When she came out again she was squinting and thoughtful.

"You say you haven't been down here."

"No." Too late now to deny it, to pretend that she had made a mistake.

"Not at all?"

"No."

"Swear."

"Bugger," Ellen said, obediently.

"Naaah, not that sort of swearing," Kasey said in exasperation. "Like an oath."

Ellen had once been a Brownie for about six weeks. "I promise on my honour—"

"Like on telly. I swear by Almighty God that I haven't been down here since last time and don't cross your fingers."

Whether you believed in God or not it was a solemn oath. On the other hand, Kasey had not worded it very carefully in her urgency. It was perfectly true; Ellen had not been down here since the last time she had been down here, and Kasey was not to know when that was. This must be what they called an escape clause. It felt like cheating.

"I swear by Almighty God that I haven't been down here since last time."

"And I haven't touched the lady."

No escape clause from that. "What's she got to do with it?" Ellen said, playing for time.

"Never mind that. Swear."

"I never touched the lady." It was a separate swear. Ellen crossed her fingers this time, even though it was the shell she had touched, not the statue. "Why shouldn't I touch her?"

"I just wanted to make sure," Kasey said. She stepped away from the fence, letting the

86

ivy drop back into place. Ellen seized her chance and made a grab at the falling stems.

"So what's wrong?"

"Whaddya mean, wrong?"

"Why did you make me swear I hadn't touched her? She's all right, isn't she? She's not got any more broken?" She made a show of patting the lady on the head and that gave her a chance to look into the shell. It was empty; the mirror had gone.

Where had it gone? Had Kasey swiped it while she had been pretending to look through the ivy? No, her hands had been in view all the time, holding the ivy out of the way.

Kasey was grinding her heel into the grass, trying to think of something to say, an answer that would satisfy Ellen.

"Don't *do* that," Ellen said.

"Do what?"

"Make marks and stomp on things. You want Mrs Sayer to know we've been here?"

"You sure she doesn't know?"

"She will if you keep mashing things up."

Kasey stopped grinding and did what Ellen had done the evening before, put the grass straight, unwinding it where she had screwed it into a mini-crop circle.

"I want you to do something for me," Kasey said. "Have you got something really nice, something you really like?"

Ellen could think of lots of things but she

did not like to say so when Kasey had so few.

"What sort of things?"

"Jewels."

"*Jewels?*" Ellen said, thinking of diamond rings.

"Well, sort of shiny things."

"I've got a bracelet." It was a twisted silver bangle like a Saxon torc. She never wore it because she did not like bracelets all that much. She could not even remember where it came from, who had given it to her.

"Give it to our lady."

"What? What'd she want it for?"

Kasey's eyes glittered. "Go on. *Please*. Just sort of lend it to her."

Ellen knew what happened to things that were loaned to the lady with iron bones, or rather, she did not know.

"Why?"

"Sort of experiment."

"All right. I'll get it later."

"No, now," Kasey said. "Get it now. Give it to her."

"Don't you trust me?"

"Of course I do," Kasey said. "Please. Get it now."

Ellen went under the hedge and up the garden. Mum would not be home for ages. If only she would turn up now so that Ellen would have an excuse not to take this charade any farther.

Please let Mum come home early. Again, that question; who was she asking?

It hardly mattered. Whoever it was took no notice, or was not listening.

The bracelet was in the drawer of her bed-side cabinet in a fancy box where she kept special things that Granny had given her, things that had belonged to Granny's grandmother: a big heavy cross made of black wood that she hoped was ebony because it sounded rich and glamorous, another of thinnest tortoiseshell so that looking through it was like gazing at the sunset, a thick metal chain, beads and brooches set with stones that might be precious.

"Semi-precious," Granny had said. "Diamonds, emeralds, sapphires and rubies are precious stones. Opals and topazes, garnets and tourmalines; they're called semi-precious. Though this lot's more likely semi-demi-precious."

And there was a ring so small that you could not believe it had ever fitted a grown-up finger, although Granny said that it had; she remembered her own auntie wearing it.

It was a good thing that Kasey did not know about this lot or the lady with iron bones would be thinking that Christmas had come early. Ellen had never shown her the hoard because it would seem like showing off. Anything else she would have offered to share, but not these.

She took out the bracelet which was at the bottom of the box, not one of Granny's gifts. Suddenly it looked pretty, desirable. Suppose Mum asked where it had gone? She had never mentioned it before, it would be bad luck if she suddenly thought of it now. Luck – or just deserts for giving away something that had been given to her? She ran her fingers through the contents of the box; what about the brooch? No, that might be an opal stuck in the middle. Stay with the bracelet, at least that really was hers. When Granny gave her the box she had said, laughing, "You'll be able to hand these on to *your* grandchildren."

That settled it. She had a *duty* to hang on to them. They were not really Ellen's at all, she was just looking after them while they were in her keeping, like the Crown Jewels that were older than the Queen who wore them, and would still be there when the Queen died, passed on to somebody else or put in the Tower of London. And she could add things of her own, such as the bracelet. No, the lady would have to do without that. There must be *something* else that would do for the lady.

As she stood by the window, looking down into the box, sifting the contents and listening to their metallic shuffling, a movement caught the corner of her eye, like Zara's fairy, off to one side, seen when not looked at. Down in the garden next door Mrs Sayer was carrying a colander full of potato peelings towards the rubbish heap. Ellen froze. Mrs Sayer was walking very slowly, apparently admiring the plants that grew on either side of the path.

Where was Kasey, what was she doing? Ellen stood upright and waved frantically on the off chance that Kasey might be standing somewhere that gave her a view of the bedroom window. She jabbed downwards with an exaggeratedly pointed finger towards Mrs Sayer, but she was still looking towards that leafy haze beyond the rubbish heap, trying to see Kasey, so it was with a shock that she saw that Mrs Sayer had turned round and was watching her with interest. Ellen, without thinking, made her scything hand grip the curtain and pull it farther back as if that was what she had been doing all the time, but Mrs Sayer had turned away and was snicking dead heads off a rose bush with her thumbnail.

As she had done yesterday Ellen crouched on the bed, with one eye trained on Mrs Sayer who continued to amble down the path. She seemed to be going slower and slower. At least Kasey would have a chance to duck under the hedge or through the fence, and escape; up the apple tree, even, if only she could be warned of the danger she was in.

At last Mrs Sayer reached the rubbish heap. She swept the colander up and jerked it down so that the potato peels went on rising and then fell, scattering over the top of the heap. *Where was Kasey?* She had not appeared from under the hedge; she must still be there if she had not got out the other way, through the fence, on to the field, but Mrs Sayer calmly shook out the last of the potato peels and walked away from the rubbish heap, back up the path, rather more quickly than she had walked down it, swinging the colander.

Ellen rose up cautiously, ears pricked and listening for the sound of Mrs Sayer's back door closing. Then she ran through the kitchen and downstairs, out on to the path. She kept right beside the hedge in spite of the thorns and when she reached the gap she looked under it first before scurrying through.

There was no sign of Kasey, but she heard a snort and the ivy trembled and parted, to reveal Kasey lurking underneath, pressed up against the lady with iron bones.

"You're mad," Ellen said. "Suppose she'd come and looked?"

"Why should she?" Kasey said. "She couldn't see me – but I could see her. If she'd got any closer I'd have gone through the fence while she was coming round the tree. Or jumped out at her whoooooooooooo, like that." Kasey sprang from the ivy, arms raised, fingers clawing.

"Keep quiet. Didn't you see me waving?"

"No. Is that it?"

"Is that what? Is what it?"

"The bracelet."

Ellen had forgotten the bracelet. While she had been kneeling on the bed, watching Mrs Sayer, she had been fumbling at it nervously with her fingertips. At some point she had slid it on to her wrist. Now she had time to remember how, before she had seen Mrs Sayer with the colander, she'd been thinking that she did not want to give her bracelet to the lady with iron bones. She had just decided that she would not substitute it with anything of Granny's, but she was almost sure that she had been about to think of something else.

It was too late now. Kasey was staring hungrily at the bracelet.

"It's like those things we saw in the museum."

"Torcs."

"Yeah, whatever. Roman?"

"Saxon."

"That isn't, though."

"Of course it's not. But it's silver."

"*Real* silver?" Kasey was easing it off Ellen's wrist. "It's pretty, isn't it?"

"Whyn't you give her some more flowers? She'd be just as happy with flowers, I bet."

"Don't you want her to have this?"

"Well ... she doesn't give things back, does she?"

Kasey's eyes snapped. "Whaddyamean?"

Ellen spotted her mistake immediately. Officially she did not know that Kasey had already given the lady a pair of imitation pearl and gilt earrings and a handbag mirror, and that the lady seemed to have accepted them.

"Well, how *can* she give things back?" Ellen saw a way out. "It'll just stay there and get all black and horrible."

"Stay where?" Kasey returned the service.

"Er ... round her neck? It won't go anywhere else."

"It will." Because of the way the lady had been cast, with her shell and drapery, she had only one free elbow. Kasey, evidently satisfied that Ellen knew nothing, eased the ends of the torc apart and slid them round the concrete arm. "Look, I'll tell you a secret. But you mustn't tell anyone else, ever."

Ellen was afraid that she was going to be made to swear again, but Kasey had gone beyond that. "This isn't the first thing I've given her."

"No? Oh, the rose," Ellen said, seeing she was safe.

"After the rose," Kasey said. "And that was only like for a present."

"What's my bracelet for, then?"

"No, listen, you know I didn't have my earrings the other day."

"You haven't got them now."

"I'll tell you why. I gave them to the lady."

"But she hasn't got any ears – well, she has, I expect, but they're under her hair."

"I didn't put them *on* her. I put them in her shell. And when I went back next day, they'd *gone*."

"Gone where?"

"Just gone. She'd taken them."

Still trying to sound innocent Ellen said, "Who? Mrs Sayer?" Up to that very second it had never occurred to her that it might indeed be Mrs Sayer who was taking the lady's presents, but—

"Of course not. She doesn't even know she's here. The lady took them."

"How could she? Kasey, she's made of *concrete*. Like garden gnomes."

"She's *not* like a garden gnome," Kasey said, furiously. "Anyway, what about those Holy Virgins and plaster Jesuses, then? People pray to them. They light candles."

"Yeah, well, they don't *take* the candles, do they? They don't come down and blow them out."

"Well, it doesn't matter what they do, does it?" Kasey said. "Because they don't do anything. I prayed and prayed and prayed about Kray and I went up the church like you said and nobody did anything. First thing I asked *her*—" Kasey actually put a protective arm around the lady's shoulders— "first time I asked her, she did it."

"She hasn't done it yet."

"She has – what do you mean?"

In that moment Ellen saw how fragile Kasey's faith must be. Kasey did not want to be reminded that so far the lady had delivered only a telephone call; Kray himself was yet to arrive. The lady must not be allowed to think for one minute that Kasey was not grateful, she must be bribed and bribed again.

"She's started doing it," Ellen conceded.

"Yes, well…" Kasey fidgeted with the bracelet on the lady's arm. "Looks silly, doesn't it?" She slipped it off again and laid it reverently in the bowl. "That's where she likes things."

"Why, what else have you given her?" Ellen slipped in, easily.

"A mirror."

"A mirror like you hang on the wall?" Ellen said, knowing perfectly well.

"Naaah, it was like out of a handbag. I – I borrowed it."

"Why don't you give her the handbag as well – and some lippy."

"It was just something nice for her – and don't make jokes, not where she can hear."

It was pointless to say that the lady could not hear. If they couldn't make jokes in front of her it would soon be dangerous to say anything at all in case she took offence and aborted her plans for returning Kray to his family. It surely would not do to voice any more doubts about whether or not she really could do anything.

"And promise you won't come back after I've gone and nick the bracelet."

"How can I nick it? It's mine."

"No." Kasey turned and arranged the bracelet more artistically in the shell. "It's hers." Her lips went on moving but Ellen could not hear what she said. This was between Kasey and the lady with iron bones. Ellen retreated to the apple tree from where she could still catch glimpses of Mrs Sayer's garden when the wind shifted the hop leaves, and, more importantly, the bit of paving by the back door which anyone would have to cross on their way down the garden.

If only it were not something so important that Kasey was asking for. It was hardly a *thing* at all, not like Zara's Barbie kitchen. Why couldn't she stick to wishing? People at school were always wishing, Ellen did it herself sometimes, and when they wished it was always for what they knew they would not get, like meeting a certain pop star or footballer, or growing up to be a pop star or a footballer. But that was all they ever did: wish. They never actually did anything about it, so they were never surprised when nothing happened. Ellen could not imagine how Kasey would feel if the lady with iron bones failed her.

CHAPTER SEVEN

Only after Kasey had gone home did Ellen remember her thoughtless remark about Mrs Sayer, thoughtless because, until she said it, she had not known that she was even thinking of Mrs Sayer.

It was the obvious explanation, that Mrs Sayer was quietly removing the gifts that Kasey left for the lady; but why quietly? Why had she not said anything? If she was asking herself where these objects were coming from the first answer she would come up with was, *That child next door, Ellen Downie,* which would also mean that she knew about Ellen making free with the end of her garden. It was quite some time since Ellen had met Mrs Sayer face to face, in the street, long before Kasey had begun worshipping her birdbath, but why had Mrs Sayer not been round to complain, or at least to ask questions?

Perhaps she was mad. Old people went a bit mad sometimes. Not Granny, of course, but Mrs Sayer looked a lot older than Granny. She might well think that she had fairies at the bottom of the garden, or ghosts. Ellen had once hoped that she would think it was ghosts.

If she was as mad as that Ellen saw no reason why she should get the bracelet as well as the earrings and the mirror. Ellen could go and fetch it now. After all, Kasey evidently expected it to disappear. It would be deceiving Kasey – was that any worse than letting Kasey deceive herself?

The thought of doing it made her uneasy. The bracelet was her own, she was entitled to take it, but how would she feel when she had done it? Probably like that time when she had raided the fragile cardboard charity collecting box that Mum kept on the fridge for loose change. It had arrived flat-packed and unfolded into the shape of a little house with a slot in the roof. Occasionally Mum emptied it and sent off the money to whatever the charity was. There were only initials on the box: AFTOL.

It was very easy to prise open without leaving any traces. She had done it only twice, and taken only thirty pence each time, but she still felt bad about it. Who was she stealing from? AFTOL had never actually had the money; was it from them or from Mum? At the time she had told herself that the box was a kind of no man's land and while the money was in it, it belonged to nobody. She had had a similar thought when she investigated the White Elephant box in the stockroom – not that she had stolen anything or even thought of it – but while the donations were in the box, no one owned them.

Then she stood quite still and really did think that her heart had stopped for one beat. That was where she had seen the handbag mirror before, in the White Elephant box. Kasey must have thought of no man's land too.

Mum was in her bedroom, on the computer. Almost without meaning to Ellen went down the stairs and out into the garden. Hanging about on the patch of lawn by the hedge, she thought what a risk Kasey had taken, borrowing the mirror. Mrs Bean would call it stealing. Now it had been stolen again.

She wondered if Kasey had found anything else among the white elephants. Probably not, that was why she had asked for the bracelet, but what was she going to ask for next? Ellen was determined not to part with anything else, especially not anything of Granny's. Why couldn't Kasey have more friends, one other friend at least, someone else to share her idol with? Why couldn't she be friends with someone like Zara Fisher who would be perfectly happy lending the lady bits of tinsel and Barbie jewellery?

Thinking of the horrible tat that she had at last thrown out only the other day, Ellen knew that Kasey would never be satisfied with anything like that. Only the best for Kasey's lady, however coy and flirty she might look with her sidelong, upturned gaze. Kasey was afraid of offending her.

Half under the hedge now, she argued with herself. If she took back the bracelet she too might offend the lady who might take it out on Kasey, which was ridiculous, but that did not stop her thinking it.

When she looked behind the ivy though, she saw that she could have saved herself all that soul-searching. The bracelet had gone.

All through the weekend she seemed to be thinking of Kasey every moment, Kasey counting the days, the hours, losing heart as each one crept away into evening, night, till the last despairing minute when Sunday became Monday and she would know that Kray was not coming back after all.

She could not make herself go round to the Carters'. More than once she started to pick up the phone, then stopped, imagining how Kasey and her mum would think it might be Kray. But on Sunday evening she decided that she had to know. She was about to climb off the bed, from where she had been watching the next-door garden for the last hour, when the phone rang.

Then Mum called, "It's for you!"

"Who is it?"

But Mum had gone back into the living room and the handset was lying on its side under the phone on the wall. Ellen advanced awkwardly and picked it up. "Hullo?"

"Guess what!" It was Kasey.

"What?"

"He's here." Kasey could hardly speak for excitement. "Kray's here. He came home."

"Oh, good," Ellen said. She ought to be shrieking and whooping and jumping around, that was the way to receive good news, but she had a feeling it might not be so good for her.

"Go and thank her," Kasey said.

"Do what?"

"Go and say thank you to the lady. Tell her I'll be round as soon as I can."

Kasey hung up. Ellen stood leaning against the work surface, listening to the electronic hooting on the line. The Carters' telephone was in their hall, which seemed chill and bare even at this time of year. She thought of Kasey rushing to it, frantic to share her wonderful news that had come almost at the last minute. Fancy having a moment to think of thanking the lady with iron bones for sending Kray back – no, that was not the reason. Not content with giving the lady a rose, a pair of earrings, a handbag mirror and a silver bracelet, Kasey was now anxious that the lady should know she was grateful. There was still the gnawing fear in her that unless the lady was kept happy she would vengefully undo all the good that Kasey thought she had done. How long was all this going to go on? It was like blackmail, only Kasey was blackmailing herself.

Ellen ran down to the end of the garden, put her head under the hedge and hissed, "Kasey says thank you very much," and felt relieved when she had done it, instead of embarrassed, which was what she ought to have been feeling, kneeling in the mud and talking to a concrete birdbath that she could not even see.

Wasn't all praying talking to something that you could not see? That was why you needed a statue...

Going back to the house, she recalled Kasey's remarks about statues of saints; candles. You didn't have to keep giving them things, you just had to let them know they were appreciated. Ellen was not at all sure how one got to be a saint. Obviously by being dead, but there had to be more to it than that. Grandpa was dead, he wasn't a saint. And the lady with iron bones had never even been alive.

That would not bother Kasey.

The flat was short of storage space and

everything that had no special place of its own ended up in the cupboard under the sink. Ellen went quietly up the stairs and into the kitchen, knelt down and opened the left-hand door. Somewhere in here, she was sure, Mum kept candles, not the fancy coloured scented ones that came out only at Christmas, but the plain white kind, for power failures.

The cupboard was due for its annual clear-out and Ellen wormed her hand very carefully among the shoe brushes, tins, boxes, bits of things that had come apart and could not be put together again, useful jars that would never be used. If she started an avalanche among this lot Mum would hear and might ask what she was looking for.

"Candles?" Mum would say, if she told the truth. "Whatever for?"

The truth would end there. Ellen could not possibly tell her.

At the back of the middle shelf her fingers discovered a flat cardboard box and eased it out. It did not contain proper candles but something even better, the little round flat kind, each in its own container, that she remembered from when she was really young – night-lights.

She had stayed alone with Granny once, and Granny had left her a night-light at bedtime. It had sat in a saucer of water on the mantel-piece, casting a golden glow up the wall.

Granny had given Mum some and said they were completely safe, but Mum was afraid of the fire risk and had never used them. These must be the very same ones.

One of these would sit nicely in the lady's seashell, and out of doors there would be no fire risk. You could leave them burning and they lasted for hours.

Mum left for work at eight o'clock in the morning for an eight-thirty start, but she had to cycle all the way into town and out the other side. Ellen could get to school in five minutes and left at eight forty.

She always watched the clock for the last few minutes, knowing from experience that even one minute could make a difference between being on time and having to endure Mrs Bean saying, "Isn't it strange how the people who live nearest to the school are always the latest?"

She did not say that, naturally, on the days when Kasey was even later.

At eight thirty-seven there was a buzz from the doorbell. Ellen was on her way out of the kitchen at the top of the stairs, and hesitated. Mum told her never to answer the door when she was out, but as she was going out herself it would not matter and in any case it was most likely the postman with something too large to go through the letterbox.

It was Kasey. Ellen stared at her.

"Yes?"

"Don't look so gobsmacked," Kasey said. "Guess where I've been."

"To see the lady?" Ellen stepped out and closed the door behind her.

"Yes. And guess what."

Ellen would have found so much guessing fatiguing at this time of the morning, only there was really no guesswork involved. "The bracelet's gone."

"How did you know?" Kasey looked offended, as if Ellen had no business finding out first.

"Because it had gone when I went out last night, to say thank you. Like you told me to." She did not bother to mention that it had disappeared on Friday, almost as soon as Kasey had left it.

"It worked." Kasey hugged herself. "She did it."

"You shouldn't go down our garden without asking," Ellen said, cattily.

"I never. I came through the fence – *up* the garden," Kasey said. "Don't you want to know about Kray?"

Not much, was Ellen's private response. What was there to know about Kray? He had gone away. He had come back. He himself did not matter, beyond the effect he had on his family. Almost she could blame him for the

106

lady with iron bones cult, except that this would be stretching things a bit.

"Is he all right?" she said, instead.

"*Yes*." Kasey was beaming. "You'll never guess why he came back."

"I thought the lady was supposed to have done that."

"She reminded him. He suddenly remembered he had to sign on today."

"Sign what?"

"Down the Dole Office."

"Is that all?" Ellen realized that at the back of her mind, she had been picturing Kray alone in the dark dank streets of Birmingham, suddenly struck by a shaft of golden light which was his bright idea about nicking the pub section out of Yellow Pages. Then the light led him to his father in the pub and finally nudged him into thinking that he must go home to his mum. And after all, it was only the thought of his dole cheque that had sent him back.

"*All?*" Kasey said. "It's brilliant. It was his dad told him to come back. They had a real barney, he said, and then they had lots of talks and his dad said if he couldn't get a job he ought to go back to school and Kray said he wasn't going back to that dump no way, and his dad said he ought to try the FE."

"What's that?"

"College of Further Education," Kasey said, in a worldly way. "So, he's going down there this afternoon to see about starting next year."

"Great. Look, we're going to be late," Ellen said. "Really late. You can tell me the rest on the way." She started down the path before Kasey could suggest another quick visit to the lady with iron bones.

Kasey continued talking, unstoppably, all the way up the hill, about how Kray was going to finish getting his GCSEs because he only had four – Ellen was surprised to know that it was that many – then he was going to do A levels and maybe University…

At this rate Kray would have the Nobel Prize before they got to school.

"He won't be earning anything, though, will he?" Ellen said, dampeningly. "And who's going to look after Mac?"

"It's going to be all right, I know it is," Kasey said. "Mum's been getting up on time – and going out. Why d'you think I'm so early?"

"*Were* early," Ellen said. "The first bell's ringing."

"No it's not, that's somebody's phone." Unfortunately she was right. "We've got to find something extra special for the lady now. Everything's going so well."

Ellen's heart sank further. Everything would go well as long as the lady was kept happy. Kray would get himself educated, Mrs Carter would get better, Mac would walk and talk, and all the while the lady would stand sinis-

terly at the end of Mrs Sayer's garden demand-
ing more and more tributes, bigger and better
presents. She remembered her own bright idea.

"Candles."

"You what?"

"Kasey, we can't keep on giving her things.
We haven't got anything left. Last night—"
she began to elaborate— "I was thinking,
what can we give her next, and then I thought
we could light candles to her. Like in church."

She had one of the night-lights in her pocket
and brought it out. Kasey looked unconvinced.

"It's all dirty. It's old. It's not worth anything."

"Candles in churches aren't worth anything."

"The Catholic ones are – you have to pay."

"Granny had to pay for this one – but they
don't cost much and they last for hours. Think
how nice it will look." Ellen could see it as she
spoke. "You know how dark it is under that
ivy, well, think of that little candle burning in
the shell, just that little flame and all the ivy
hanging down. If the lady's got candles burning we won't have to keep giving her things.
There's ten of these in the box."

Kasey was thinking it over. "*How* long do
they last?"

"All night, I think."

"We'd have to keep one going all the time.
We could time the first one and then make
sure we were always ready with the next

before it went out."

"I bet they don't burn non-stop in church," Ellen said, seeing what she had let herself in for: endless vigils, an endless supply of candles. "*That's* the bell."

They ran the last few yards to the gate and across the playground, caught up in the stream of people heading for the door, while the infants trotted off round the side to their mobiles that lined the edge of the playground.

The classroom was half full as they went in. They both prepared a smug smile and flashed it towards Mrs Bean's desk, but there was no one to receive it. The desk, which was usually half occupied by Mrs Bean's large handbag and even larger work bag, was clear. Mrs Bean was not there.

"Give *her* one for being late," Ellen said, as they went to their table. One or two people went to look in the corridor and others milled around aimlessly. Mrs Bean always made such a fuss about their being silent when they came in and sat down that Ellen expected a riot to break out – fights, splintering furniture, shattered light bulbs – but people sat down quietly as they usually did, eyeing the door uncertainly as if suspecting that Mrs Bean had laid a trap for them and, if they misbehaved, would leap out of hiding crying, "Ha! Gotcha!"

In the end Mrs Booker looked in, asked if anyone had seen Mrs Bean and went away again. Mr Lewis arrived to take the register.

"Where's Mrs Bean?" someone said.

"Got held up in traffic, I expect," Mr Lewis said. "Or she might be ill. That does happen to us as well, you know," he said, when people made incredulous noises. "I've even been known to take a day off myself. And none of you noticed, I bet, you heartless creatures. Well, be on your best behaviour. If Mrs Bean is off sick we're going to have to double up somewhere because I've got to go to a meeting later on."

Ellen was wishing that Mr Lewis could be their class teacher because they were behaving just as well for him as they did for Mrs Bean and he had not snapped at them once, when Emily's mother, the school secretary, put her head round the door and made urgent signs.

"Get yourselves into assembly, you know the drill," Mr Lewis said, going out with her.

Ellen looked across at Kasey to say what a nice day they would have without Mrs Bean, and saw Kasey's expression. Kasey was obviously thinking very hard, but without the usual side effects of rubbing her head, sucking her teeth or breathing heavily to prove it. Instead she was staring at nothing, her frown reduced to one single downstroke above her left eye. Her mouth was slightly open and when Marsha, who sat nearest to the door and could see the Year 5s go by, stood up and waved to the rest to follow her down the corridor to the hall, Kasey did not move.

Ellen nudged her as she stood up. "You all right? Come on." Kasey rose, without saying anything, and they tagged on to the end of the line.

The hall was awash with that seaside noise of people not making a noise, a kind of swishing, echoing sound like water on shingle. The teachers usually sat opposite their classes, but they were in a huddle, talking, until Mr Lewis came in and went to the front.

"I'm afraid I've got some bad news," he said. "Mrs Bean has had an accident."

Most people made a sound, mainly of surprise, because teachers did not have accidents, but Ellen felt Kasey beside her give a little jump. Even though she was sitting on the floor cross-legged, like everyone else, her whole body seemed to jolt, as if she had received an electric shock.

"As you know … well, I don't suppose you did know," Mr Lewis went on, unhappily. He too seemed shocked. "Mrs Bean has to drive a long way to school in the mornings. As she was leaving home today a neighbour's son lost control of his bike and fell in front of her car, and she collided with another vehicle when she tried to avoid him."

People began to take in that this was not just interesting news and a nice break from routine, but something awful, injury, even death perhaps. The whole hall was quiet as they started to sort out how they felt about it.

Mr Lewis was saying, "Mrs Bean had her son in the car. They've both been injured, although not seriously, but the other boy is very badly hurt. I think we should all pray for his safe recovery."

Necks bowed, hands clasped themselves together. Beside Ellen, Kasey gave a little sigh. Ellen looked round. Kasey's pale face was yellow-white with ugly brown shadows under her eyes and round her mouth. Her hands were raised halfway to her chin, curled like claws.

Mr Lewis had started to pray but Ellen stood up and leaned over to touch Miss Hoskins on the arm. "Miss, I think Kasey's going to be sick. Can I—"

"Yes, quick," Miss Hoskins said, seeing Kasey's face.

Kasey was still sitting. Ellen hauled her to her feet and towards the door, desperate to get to the lavatory before Kasey threw up on the vinyl tiles and Mr Samson had to come and clean up. She half dragged her down the corridor, but before they reached the cloakroom Kasey's legs gave way and she leaned against the wall, slipping down it to sit on the floor. She was muttering over and over again, "It's my fault. It's my fault. She did it. She did it. *She* did it."

CHAPTER EIGHT

Ellen watched the door of the hall, but it stayed shut. No one came out. They were alone, just the two of them, in all that shiny silent length of corridor, Kasey sitting on the floor, doubled up, back against the wall, Ellen standing over her, not knowing what to do.

"Look, come in the toilet anyway," Ellen said, "even if you're not sick. Or there'll be teachers and everything..." Much as she wanted a teacher to take charge she knew that it would be the last thing Kasey wanted.

Kasey was shivering, still that nasty blotchy-white colour like paper towels, and still muttering, "It was my fault."

"Come *on*." Ellen kept tugging at her hand until Kasey unfolded and crawled upright, hands flat to the wall. She put an arm around her and steered her towards the girls' toilets, but when they reached the coat racks Kasey collapsed on a bench. "Do you want some water?"

Kasey shook her head and sat with her hair hanging forward to hide her face, hands gripping the edge of the bench on either side. The coat racks were open to the corridor, but at least they were more private here than sitting out there on the floor. Ellen sat down beside Kasey, holding her hand, until Kasey took a great gulp of air and began to cry.

Kasey never cried. She raged and sulked and scowled, but Ellen had not seen her in tears before. And to make it worse, she did not know why she was crying. It could not only be because she was sorry for Mrs Bean and her son whose name, they all knew, was Tim, and the unknown, unnamed boy who had fallen from his bike and was worst hurt of all.

My fault. She did it. Who had done what?

"I never meant it," Kasey sniffed. She was getting a hold of herself again.

"Never meant what?"

"About Mrs Bean."

"Oh." Ellen saw. Kasey was as fond of Mrs Bean as Mrs Bean was of Kasey, and out of Mrs Bean's hearing Kasey had always been very free with her comments, threats and insults. Well, it was hard on Mrs Bean, having an accident, but that did not cancel out how mean she had always been to Kasey. "You don't have to feel sorry. I mean, you can feel sorry for her but you don't have to feel sorry about hating her."

"I asked the lady," Kasey whispered.

"What? What did you ask her?"

"When I gave her things, I asked her. Let Kray come back. Make Mum better. Make something horrible happen to Mrs Bean."

Ellen had not seen. She had got it all wrong. Kasey had not simply been asking the lady with iron bones for favours, she had been seeking revenge, and now she had got it.

"Kasey, don't be daft. That old statue, she can't do anything. You've imagined it. It wasn't her who made Kray come back, and your mum—"

"It was, it was." Kasey ground her teeth together. "No one else did anything, and I asked and asked, but when I asked *her* it happened, and I gave her all those things and now she's done this. Suppose that other boy dies. It'll be my fault."

"You're mad," Ellen said. "You didn't ask her to kill anybody, did you?"

"I wanted Mrs Bean to be hurt and she had her accident because that boy fell off his bike. Well, if he dies I suppose Mrs Bean will go to prison or something, but I don't want him to die."

"I don't suppose she'll even go to prison," Ellen said, absently. "It doesn't sound like it was her fault, does it?" She had put her arm

116

around Kasey and, very slowly, Kasey was calming down, but at the word "fault" she began to shake again.

"No, it wasn't her fault, it was mine. What shall I do?"

"Well, don't tell anyone," Ellen said. If a grown-up heard what Kasey had just told her, men in white coats would come.

"We've got to make her change it," Kasey said. "We've got to ask her to make that boy all right. And Tim," she added as an afterthought. "He hasn't done anything. He can't help what his mum's like. Let's go now."

"Go where?"

"Down yours. To see the lady."

"Siddown!" Ellen rapped, as Kasey started to her feet. "You *are* mad. We can't go now. Miss Hoskins knows we're out here. Assembly'll be over in a minute and she'll come and find us. We'll get into ever such trouble if we go out of school. And you'll have to tell people why you bunked off. Do you want to do that?" she added craftily.

On cue the door of the hall opened and the infants started to come out. As they passed the cloakroom benches they all turned, eyes right, to stare at Ellen and Kasey in that blank, cheerful way that infants have; rather like sheep. Kasey, recovering her spirits slightly, glared back at them with her basilisk gaze and one or two turned pink and began to grizzle. The

Reception Class was followed by the Year 1s and then the Year 2s. With them came Miss Beckett. She stopped when she reached the coat racks and sat down on the opposite bench.

"Feeling better?" she said. "Poor old Kasey, was it something you'd eaten? I saw you rush out, you did look ill."

Kasey's jaw dropped slightly at these sympathetic words and the kindly tone. Perhaps Miss Beckett was chastened by the fate of Mrs Bean and afraid that lightning would strike her. If she only knew...

"You've been crying. Did you have a pain?"

"Yes, Miss. It's all right now. I've been ever so sick," Kasey said.

"Yes, ever so. All her breakfast," Ellen said, piling it on.

"Do you want to go and lie down? Would you rather go home?"

Kasey sensed safety in numbers. "No, thank you, Miss. I'm all right."

"Well, you take it easy. If you feel ill again tell your teacher right away. I'm not sure who it will be today. All right?"

She stood up and went after her class who were already showing signs of going astray during that long journey across the playground to their mobile.

"What's got into her?" Kasey said, ungratefully.

"Do you really feel all right now?" Ellen said. Kasey was not exactly rosy, but her skin was skin coloured again and those horrible bruises had faded. The shock was wearing off.

"Better," Kasey said. "Look, we got to do something about that boy. We got to see the lady."

"He'll be in intensive care, I expect," Ellen said, thinking of all the hospital programmes she had seen on television. "He'll be all right for now. Look, come on in the classroom before anyone else starts asking questions."

When everyone was in the Year 6 room, Mr Lewis came in, frowning. "As I feared," he said, "we're going to have to divide you up – no, Kyle, not with a saw. Leave it out, will you? I'm not in the mood. Now, pay attention. Everyone on this side of me will please go and join Year 5 for the first half of the morning. The rest of you stay here and Year 4 will join *you*. Is that clear?"

Immediately a small panic erupted as all those in the middle of the room put up their hands to ask which side they were on. As Mr Lewis started to go through it again, with hand signals, Ellen had a daring idea, so daring that for a moment she could scarcely believe she was having it. It was not the kind of idea she usually had. She was not a teacher's lick, but she supposed that she was a good girl. She never got jumped on like Kasey, on the assumption that she *must* be doing something wrong, one of the usual suspects. She was not a plotter or a planner, she did not need to be. Things usually turned out the way she wanted, and if they did not, it didn't matter terribly. All that was about to change.

"*Now* is it clear?" Mr Lewis was saying. "After break we'll have you all in the hall with Year 5 for music. Kasey, I saw you looking very seedy in assembly. Are you all right now?"

"Sir," Kasey said, and Mr Lewis had known Kasey long enough to understand that this meant, "Yes, thank you very much, kind of you to ask."

People were beginning to leave, and others to squeeze together to make room for the incoming Year 4s. Ellen stood up and nudged Kasey to join her.

"Our half's got to stay," Kasey said.

"Not us," Ellen said. "Come on, I've got an idea." They picked up their bags and followed the last person, who was Emily, out of the room.

They were almost at the Year 5 door when Emily noticed them. "You aren't with us," she said, officiously. "You're meant to stay with the little ones." She flounced her broad backside and disappeared through the doorway.

"I *said* we were in the wrong half," Kasey protested.

"No we aren't, *we're* not in any half," Ellen said. She took Kasey firmly by the elbow and kept on walking, down the last bit of corridor, out of the end door, past the refuse bins to the side gate.

"Where are we going?" Kasey said, blinking a little at Ellen's effrontery.

"Home," Ellen said. "Then we'll come back at break over the fields and no one will know we've been away. Miss Hoskins will think we've been with Year 4 and Mrs Booker will think we've been with Year 5."

"What about after we get back?"

"Didn't you hear Mr Lewis? We're doing music with Year 5, in the hall. We'll all be together again."

"But where are we going?" Kasey said. "I told you, I don't want to go home."

"We're not going to your home," Ellen said. "We're going to mine." She took the night-light out of her pocket. "We'll go and light a candle to the lady and you can ask her to make it all right about Mrs Bean. Isn't that what you wanted?"

Ellen wished she had had time to plan things more carefully. If they had absconded over the fields they could have entered Mrs Sayer's garden through the back fence. It was not Mrs Sayer she was worried about – it was Mrs Walcott, always on the lurking lookout,

121

convinced that Ellen was neglected because she was alone in the house mornings and evenings. When Mrs Walcott first moved in she had been very loud about single mothers who scrounged off welfare. When she discovered that Mum had a perfectly good job she changed her tune to single mothers who went out to work and left their children to roam all over the place and come home to empty houses. Mum smiled when they met and in private called her an interfering old haybag.

"Now listen," Ellen said, "when we get to our front hedge keep your head down so Old Mother Walcott doesn't see us."

"What about when we go up the path?"

"We won't. We'll go along the footpath and in through Mrs Sayer's fence."

The drawback to this cunning plan revealed itself when they were through the fence and Ellen had checked Mrs Sayer's garden for signs of Mrs Sayer. She took out the night-light just as Kasey was lifting the ivy. Kasey said, "What are we going to light it with?"

Ellen had not thought of that. On television people always had matches and lighters when they needed them. "There's matches in the kitchen," she said. "I'll go and get them. Wait here."

The larch-lap fence screened Ellen's end of the garden from the Walcotts' downstairs windows, but she went very quietly along the path in case a Walcott heard echoing footsteps. As quietly she turned the key in the lock and tiptoed upstairs.

The flat seemed eerie in its mid-morning emptiness; she felt as if she were trespassing in someone else's home, far more than when she was really trespassing, in Mrs Sayer's garden. Everything was just as she, the last one out, had left it. She was not meant to be here at this hour, trespassing not in space but in time. She took the box of matches from the back of the drawer under the draining board and left as quietly as she could.

As she went downstairs she could hear Mrs Walcott hoovering, through the party wall. That should keep *her* out of the way, then.

Kasey was under the ivy with the lady, kneeling in front of her. Ellen could guess what was going on because the telltale soles of Kasey's shoes were poking out.

Ellen joined her. "You can be seen. Your feet."

Kasey said nothing but shuffled forward on her knees. She was clinging to the seashell, her hands over the lady's hands, gazing up into her eyes, but the lady did not return her look. As usual her face was turned aside, smiling sidelong and upward. What have you got to smirk about? Ellen thought. But if the lady could really do all the things that Kasey thought she could do, she would have good reason to smirk.

Kasey had placed the night-light in the bowl of the seashell. Ellen handed her the matches and stood silently while Kasey struck one and lit the wick. The flare of the match branded her eye with a bright white splash, that turned to red and then faded to show the lady's ivy grotto softly illuminated, the little flame burning steadily in its windless shelter. Kasey, still kneeling, clasped her hands one over the other on the rim of the shell, bent her head.

Praying, Ellen thought. Perhaps she ought to do the same, partly to keep Kasey company, because Kasey would like it, and partly because it might just do some good. She stamped on that thought at once. How could it possibly do any good? And she did not at all care for the sight of the lady now. Lit from below she had a demonic look, her eyes long and heavy-lidded, curving up at the corners, her mouth more sneer than smile.

Kasey showed no signs of wanting to leave. Ellen fidgeted, coughed, and then touched her on the shoulder. "We ought to get back." Kasey shrugged her off, irritably. "Look, Kasey, we don't have to stay. That's what the candle's for … to remind her of us."

Kasey raised her head, opened her eyes and looked up at the lady, but she did not see what Ellen saw. "Please," Kasey said, just once. Then she stood up, slipped through the ivy, and Ellen followed.

"Which way are we going back?"

"Up the field," Ellen said. "We can get in round behind the mobiles when break starts and then we can go to the hall and no one will know we bunked off."

"Suppose Miss Hoskins and Mrs Booker check up?" Kasey said. "They will if it's me."

"They won't if it's me," Ellen said. "No one would think I could work all this out."

"Yeah, they'll say I thought of it," Kasey said, gloomily.

"Are you feeling all right now?" Kasey looked better. The brisk walk up the fields was bringing a little colour to her face, Ellen's fiendish calculations had taken her mind off her problems for a while and, anyway, she had at least tried to undo the harm she thought she had done.

No one noticed that they had been missing. Hooray for Mrs Bean being away, Ellen thought, and then she remembered why Mrs Bean was away, and that if it hadn't been for Mrs Bean's accident they would not have needed to visit the lady with iron bones.

Kasey was very silent for the rest of the day, but people were used to that, and everybody knew that she had felt unwell at assembly, so no one nagged. During the afternoon sports practice Miss Hoskins told her to sit in the shade with a book if she did not feel like taking part. Kasey, who never felt like taking part and always gave any team she was in a hard time, agreed with as much enthusiasm as she could fake and sat on the grass eating daisies and pretending to read a book about vampires. Ellen thought that this was a mistake, not the daisies and vampires, but the chance to sit and think. She could imagine Kasey going over and over in her mind the thought of the accident, and the boy on the bicycle who had fallen in front of Mrs Bean's car so that something horrible would happen to Mrs Bean.

Surely Kasey did not truly believe that the lady had done all that, along with her other favours? But, on the other hand, they were supposed to believe all that stuff about miracles, like the loaves and the fishes in the stained-glass window, and there were people who believed in angels and flying saucers and weeping statues … and vampires. Was worshipping a birdbath all that crazy?

At home time Kasey waited while Ellen changed out of her kit.

"Win anything?"

"It was only practice. I was second in the four hundred metres and third in the long jump." And I did it all by myself, she added silently. I didn't pray to win and I didn't wish. I just ran and jumped and some people ran faster and jumped further and maybe next week when it's really sports day I won't win anything and I won't mind then because I don't mind now.

It was a pity she could not get some of this across to Kasey, but it would not make any difference; she would never understand how it felt to want something as much as Kasey did. Maybe the people who had beaten her today had been wishing and praying themselves, and that was *why* they had beaten her. Perhaps there had to be people on earth like Ellen Downie so that all the wishers and prayers would have someone to run faster than and jump further than.

"What time was it when we lit that candle?" Kasey said, as they walked down Church Road.

"About ten o'clock," Ellen said.

"And how long do they burn for?"

"I think it said five hours on the box – no, eight," she lied, thinking that five hours must be over already.

"Well, find out. Make sure you light another one as soon as ours goes out," Kasey said.

"Do you want to come and have a look now?"

"No. I think I'll go home."

"Shall I come with you?"

Kasey was looking peaky again, but she shook her head. "I don't need *watching*. You watch that candle."

The night-light wick was still burning in its little tin case at the bottom of the bowl of the seashell, but the flame quivered now, and the shadows slid nowhere more sinisterly than on the face of the lady with iron bones.

Ellen stood hidden by the ivy, watching the flame, the lady's shifting smile, and smelled the melted wax, noticed the scent of the ivy leaves that must be due to the extra warmth. It was usually cool under the ivy, but even that little flame had made a difference.

It was a shame that the lady was not made of wood, then she might suffer a nasty accident, mysteriously catching fire and reducing Ellen's problems to a heap of ash with bones of charcoal.

They were real problems now. Of course the lady had nothing to do with Mrs Bean's accident, but if that boy was really badly hurt, if he died, what would happen to Kasey, what would she do to herself, tortured with guilt, convinced that it was all her doing?

Make it all right, Ellen begged, and put her hand on the lady's shoulder. "Make it all right. Don't let him die."

And a voice said, "I think this is all getting rather out of hand, don't you?"

CHAPTER NINE

Ellen did not even jump. She stood quite still, while her heart seemed to whirr and she heard a surge of blood in her ears. Then she felt very tired, and weak, as if she had been dreading bad news and had been told it, and found that knowing was easier than dreading.

When at last she turned, the ivy curtain was lifted and there, on the other side, looking in at Ellen, was Mrs Sayer.

"I thought it was the other one," Mrs Sayer said. "I thought it was your friend who did the praying. What's her name?"

"Kasey," Ellen said, and stepped out from under the ivy to face Mrs Sayer.

"It's Kasey who leaves fashion accessories for my birdbath, then?" Mrs Sayer said. "Very kind of her, I'm sure – but I'm not at all sure about the candle. That looks too much like organized religion for my liking. As for the praying—"

"It's not like religion," Ellen said.

"Isn't it?" Mrs Sayer smiled, but sadly. "Making offerings, praying, lighting votive candles – yes, that's what they're called. If I hadn't heard you just now I might have thought that you – Kasey – had given it to her in case she was afraid of the dark, but it's not that at all, is it? What's all this about not letting him die? Have you turned my poor little Calypso into a jealous god?"

"We thought she was stuck down here because she was broken," Ellen said. "We didn't do that." She pointed to the lady's exposed shin.

"I know you didn't. Perhaps I ought to have given her a decent burial, or put her out for the bin men ... broken her up for a rockery," Mrs Sayer said.

"What did you call her – Calypso? Why?"

"What do you call her?"

"The lady with iron bones," Ellen mumbled. It sounded ridiculous.

"I'm surprised you never noticed; all those times you visited her and you didn't know her name. Look round the bottom of the pedestal."

Mrs Sayer went on holding the ivy aside. Ellen crouched and pressed down the grass and weeds around the base of the statue. There were letters, a whole word: Calypso.

"Why's she called that?"

"Don't they teach you about Greek myths at school any more? Calypso was a nymph who lived on an island in the Aegean Sea. I don't think she ever killed anyone."

Ellen was still thinking of the first thing Mrs Sayer had said. "You knew we came down here?"

"Good grief," Mrs Sayer said. "I may be old but I'm not senile. Did you think I believed I had fairies at the bottom of the garden? I've been watching *you* for two years."

"Going through the fence?"

"Of course. Why do you think I never had it mended?"

"You didn't mind?"

"You never did any damage, you didn't even steal the apples. I'd hardly have known you were here if I hadn't seen you – yes, of course I saw you. All the time. You aren't at all fairy-like, Ellen. And then, what was it – two weeks ago – someone picked a rose and left it in the shell."

"But how did you know? She's hidden under the ivy."

"*Hedera colchica.*"

"Who?"

"The ivy. That's its name. It doesn't come right down to the ground. From the rubbish heap I can see feet."

"The rose was in the shell."

"My dear child, when you were on your

131

own I only *saw* you. When Kasey is here, I can *hear* you. I heard her talking after you'd gone back through the hedge. 'This is for you,' she said. Of course I had to go and look. If they're going to start picking my flowers, I thought; but the next time I went to look I found these."

She held out her hand and in it lay the earrings.

"Why did you take them? You didn't take the rose."

"I thought at first they might have been left by accident, while you were playing a game, but the next day…" She held out her hand again. "This very nice handbag mirror. I was going to give the earrings back, the next time I saw you, but after I found the mirror I began to wonder what was going on, so I took that too."

"You shouldn't have," Ellen cried.

"Shouldn't I? Out of my own birdbath in my own garden? I think I was entitled to whatever the fairies left in it, don't you? Look, Ellen, I think I'd like to sit down, if you don't mind. I find standing rather tiring without my stick. Come over to the bench."

For the first time ever Ellen, following Mrs Sayer, walked on the cinder path that went round the edge of the rubbish heap, under the apple branches, and on to the crazy paving that crossed the lawn between the rose bushes and lavender. In all those years of creeping under the hedge, she had never before been in the real garden. Mrs Sayer walked slowly towards the terrace under her back windows and sat down on a wooden bench, patting it to show that Ellen should sit beside her.

"When does your mother come home? Five? That gives us plenty of time. Right, item number three, a silver bracelet."

"That's mine," Ellen said. "I didn't want to leave it but Kasey didn't have anything else." She looked at the things laid out in Mrs Sayer's lap: the earrings, the mirror, the bracelet. "Are you going to keep them?"

"I don't think I am," Mrs Sayer said, "but tell me, Ellen, who did you think was taking them?"

"*I* thought it was you," Ellen said. "I *did* … not at first, though. I didn't know what was going on. No, to start with, I thought Kasey was taking them herself. I think I did."

"But you never believed that the lady with iron bones was making off with them during the night?"

"My bracelet went in daytime," Ellen said, playing for time. What *had* she thought?

"So it did." Mrs Sayer smiled. "Don't you think it was rather valuable to leave out in the garden? It's solid silver. You ought to look after it. Doesn't it look better since I polished it?"

The delicate spirals gleamed so brightly they looked white. Ellen felt ashamed of letting it get dull and tarnished in the drawer.

"But those other things were Kasey's, were they? And whose idea was the votive candle?"

"It's a night-light."

"Good heavens, I know what it is, but you're using it as a votive candle. That's what it's called if you make a vow and give things to prove that you mean it, particularly if you give them to a graven image – or even a concrete one."

"It wasn't a vow," Ellen said. "Kasey wanted something."

"A bribe."

"That's what I thought. Look, she wanted something ever so badly, and she prayed in assembly and then we went up the church and prayed again, but nothing happened, and then I showed her the la— Calypso – and she said she was like a saint in church and she prayed to her instead, and gave her the rose."

"And it worked?"

"Yes," Ellen said. "That's the trouble. It did work."

"No," Mrs Sayer said, firmly. "It didn't work. Be sensible, Ellen, birdbaths do not work miracles."

"I don't believe in miracles anyway," Ellen said, "but Kasey had to. She had to believe *something* was happening."

"What was it she wanted so badly?" Mrs Sayer asked.

"You won't tell anyone?"

"I promise. Who would I tell?"

"Kray – her brother – he's her half-brother really, got fed up with being stuck at home because he hasn't got a job and their mum's not been well since Mac was born – that's her little brother. Anyway, Kray went off to Birmingham to find his dad – that's not Kasey's dad, and Kasey wanted him to come back because her mum got depressed again."

"That was what she prayed for?"

"Yes, and in the end she asked the lady and gave her the rose and then she gave her the earrings. And the next day her mum went shopping."

"That was the miracle?"

"If you knew her mum... No, the day after that her brother rang up and said he was coming home and she gave the lady the mirror, and then my bracelet; in case she changed her mind, I suppose. And he did come home, and it wasn't because of the lady at all, it was because he had to sign on for the dole on Monday, and Kasey thinks the lady reminded him about signing on. Now she's afraid that if she doesn't keep giving the lady things, she'll change her mind and make it all come undone again, and I couldn't let her go on putting jewels and stuff in the shell, so I thought of the candles. And then we got to school this morning and we found the lady had done something else."

"Hold on; slow down," Mrs Sayer said. "We?"

"Kasey."

"For someone who never moves, Calypso leads a very full life. What had she done this time?"

"It's not funny," Ellen said. "Kasey thinks she may have killed someone."

"What did she do?"

"Not Kasey – the lady."

"Oh, this is beyond a joke." Mrs Sayer looked really angry. "What is this wretched child doing to herself?"

"There's this teacher, Mrs Bean. Kasey doesn't like her. She doesn't like Kasey. She's always picking on her and making snarky remarks when Kasey's late. She's often late when her mum's ill and she has to look after Mac. Well, this morning Mrs Bean didn't come to school and Mr Lewis, the head teacher, he said she'd had an accident in her car and run over this boy on a bike. And the boy's badly hurt and we had to pray for him in assembly."

"What has this to do with Kasey?"

"She's been asking the lady, Calypso, to do something horrible to Mrs Bean."

"And she truly believes that Calypso sent a complete stranger to fall in front of Mrs Bean's car and be killed so that Mrs Bean would suffer?"

Ellen nodded.

"And what do you believe?"

"I don't believe she did it."

"But wasn't it you I heard just now, asking your lady, 'Don't let him die'?"

"I didn't mean it!"

"Oh, I think you did."

"Not like Kasey means it. I just meant I hoped he didn't die and touched the lady for good luck. I've always done that."

"Good luck's only getting what you want, isn't it? What else do you do for good luck?"

"Touch wood," Ellen said. "Cross your fingers."

"Do you know why you do that?" Mrs Sayer asked, curiously.

"Good luck…" Ellen muttered, sulkily.

"You're making the sign of the Cross," Mrs Sayer told her. "That's a Christian symbol. Shouldn't mean anything to people who aren't Christians. Why do you touch my birdbath for good luck?"

"Because she's there."

"So is the old stepladder. Why not touch the stepladder?"

"She's a person."

"No, she is a lump of iron and concrete that looks like a person."

"That's what Kasey said. She said statues in churches are just plaster and stuff, and croxes – crucers—"

"Crucifixes. People pray in front of a statue because they can see it, something to look at, it's the face of what they believe in. That's why they go to church or mosque or temple; it puts them in the same place as the thing they believe in. But what is Calypso the face of? Do you know why I'm telling you all this?"

"To keep me out of your garden?"

"I could easily do that with chicken wire. No, I'm telling *you* because I don't think it would do much good to tell your friend. Deep down, Ellen, she knows as well as you do that she is worshipping a birdbath, putting a face to what she believes in, only she doesn't know what she believes in. Do you?"

"I don't believe in *her* – the lady."

"So who were you talking to when I found you? 'Don't let him die.'"

"I don't know."

"That's the hardest thing, isn't it?" Mrs Sayer said. "The feeling that there is nobody in charge, nobody taking care, nobody putting things right. Now, Kasey has asked for something she did not really want and thinks – this is the real problem – thinks that *she* made it happen. It's called ill-wishing."

"She thinks the lady did it."

"No she doesn't. Calypso is the face of what Kasey believes in. Kasey believes in Kasey, which is an excellent thing to believe in so long as she doesn't start to imagine that she has supernatural powers."

"It's that boy on the bike. That's why she's

really upset."

"Because he had to be hurt to make her wish come true. Do you read fairy tales?"

"Not any more."

"You ought to. Think of all those stories where people get their wishes granted; something always backfires, doesn't it? Because they wish for things they shouldn't have. Kasey's got her wish and it's come true through injuring someone else, that's why she's upset. She wants to unmake it, and it's too late."

"That's awful," Ellen said.

"It is if you believe in wishing."

"What can we do?"

"Nothing yet," Mrs Sayer said, "but this dangerous nonsense has got to stop. I'm afraid we're going to have to wait and see what happens to that boy who was hurt. Did your Mr Lewis say *how* he was hurt? Head injuries?"

"I don't think so. I didn't hear everything, I had to take Kasey out of the hall. I thought she was going to be sick."

"Poor silly child. He's not a local boy? You've no way of finding out?"

"No. Mrs Bean lives in Maidstone."

"You must be patient. If he doesn't have head injuries he will probably be all right. We must hope. But Ellen, you must understand, when all this is over we have got to get rid of Calypso before she starts World War Three."

"What are you going to do to her?"

"Just now I'd happily take a hammer to her," Mrs Sayer said, "but that would be too drastic. I suppose I could fence you out, but really, Calypso has got to leave off being a goddess. If she stays where she is, collecting her tributes and candles, Kasey will be forever in her debt because the boy recovered, or trying to buy her off in case she makes something worse happen. It'll be a protection racket."

"I don't think she'll ask for anything else."

"I'm not talking about anything else, I'm thinking of what she's asked for already. Has that brother of hers ever been in trouble with the police?"

"No! Well, I don't think so."

"All right; now, suppose he goes out one night and breaks into a house, or steals a car; starts a fight? Has an accident, even. What will Kasey be saying to herself, then? 'If I hadn't asked the lady to send him back from Birmingham, this wouldn't have happened.' Do you see what I mean?"

Ellen did see, an endless future of Kasey blaming the lady or, as she now understood, blaming herself, for everything that went wrong for ever and ever.

"It all depends on this boy," Mrs Sayer said. "When we know what Calypso has done or has not done, we can act. Come and tell me at once, as soon as you know. Come up the front path and ring the doorbell, if you like. Then we can plot."

"What about the candles?"

"What are they – five-hour night-lights? We'll keep them going for now, for Kasey's sake, not Calypso's. All we can do is hope."

"Pray?"

"Are you religious?" Mrs Sayer said. "I shan't be praying, I shall simply hope. Not wish," she added, sternly. "There's to be no more wishing. That's what you were really doing, isn't it?"

"Is it?"

"Of course. Kasey didn't even dare hope that her brother would come back, or her mother would get better, or even that Mrs Bean would meet with an awful fate. You can only hope if you can do something about it, or if it's likely to happen. Otherwise you just have to wish and take the consequences when your wish comes true. You do realize, don't you," Mrs Sayer said, "that if Kasey had remembered that Kray had to sign on on Mondays, she could have hoped that he'd remember too, instead of wishing."

Mrs Bean was not in class again next morning. Mrs Booker scuttled across from Year 4 to take the register, but before they could ask her any questions there was a crash and a yell from the Year 4 room where she had left the door open, and by the time she had reached William Youngman there were sounds of a fight getting up steam. When Kasey did not answer to her name Mrs Booker, unlike Mrs Bean, made no comment.

Ellen had been watching the door from the moment she sat down. Yesterday Kasey, so bouncy and confident, had been on time, called for her like in the old days; they would have been early if Kasey had not hung around talking. Now she was not here at all. Ellen ran through all the possibilities in her mind: Kasey had run away; Kasey was in Mrs Sayer's garden right now, bending the lady's ear; Kasey was ill. It was probably the last. If her mum was better and her brother was at home, Kasey would have time to be ill for once, not an illness like flu or whooping cough, but fear. And she had been so pale and shaky that anyone would think she was having a real illness. No one could suspect her of putting it on.

When they went into the hall for assembly Mr Lewis was already standing at the front, talking to a policewoman. Ellen felt her insides give an awful lurch, as if something had come loose. For a second she knew how Kasey had felt. Everyone else was very quiet too, watching the policewoman.

This had to be something to do with Mrs Bean's accident.

CHAPTER TEN

"Oh, please," Ellen whispered. "Oh please. *Please*." The silence in the hall was so very silent that the last please was loud enough to be heard and Ellen had to turn it into a cough.

Mr Lewis turned round, then, and they all saw that he was holding a cycling helmet. He suddenly noticed how nervous and quiet they were, and placed the helmet on his head. It was too small and perched there like a large blue beetle, rocking to and fro. A wave of relief rolled across the hall, over Ellen. Mr Lewis would never have done that if he had bad news; it would be like going to a funeral wearing a red nose. He swept off the helmet again, bowed and waved to them to sit down. No one quite dared to laugh but the policewoman was smiling.

"First the good news," Mr Lewis said. "Actually, there's no bad news. Doesn't that make a nice change?"

Ellen realized that he was feeling relieved, too, and wished that Kasey were sitting in her usual place beside her, slowly understanding, as everyone else was starting to understand, that the good news must have something to do with the accident.

"What is this?" Mr Lewis was twirling the helmet on one finger. "A cycling helmet. Absolutely right. How many of you cycle to school?"

A number of hands went up.

"How many of you wear one of these?" All the hands stayed up. "Of course; you aren't allowed to cycle to school unless you wear one. Now, how many of you wear yours when you *aren't* cycling to school?"

The hands began to waver and people started looking round at other people to see if it were safe to tell the truth. "All right, don't perjure yourselves. The point is this, the boy who collided with Mrs Bean's car yesterday was wearing a helmet. If he hadn't been he would have received serious head injuries. As it is, he's broken his leg and acquired a few nasty dents, but he's not in any danger. The bike is a write-off but the important thing is, what could have been a dreadful accident with loss of life, has turned out to have a happy ending after all. Mrs Bean and Tim have only minor injuries and the other lad will be out of hospital in a day or two. WPC Dale was coming in to give us a talk on road safety anyway, but I hope you'll listen to her even more carefully now."

Perhaps it was just as well that Kasey wasn't there. Ellen knew what she would have been saying: "The lady did it," and what she would have been thinking: What do I give the lady now?

They stood up again to sing a hymn, and said the Lord's Prayer, but Ellen scarcely noticed. When WPC Dale began to speak she did not hear a word. If only she could get the news to Kasey at once. She dared not bunk off school again and she would not be allowed out at lunch time. Perhaps she could telephone, if she asked someone very nicely, but if she did that, what could she say? She did not imagine that Kasey had confided in anyone at home. She would be in bed, feeling ill, miserable, desperate, convinced that she had perhaps killed somebody by – what had Mrs Sayer called it? – ill-wishing. If Ellen rang up it might be Mrs Carter who answered the phone and if she said, "Tell Kasey that boy's going to be all right," her mum might start wondering what Kasey had been doing.

And she wanted to be completely sure before she said anything. After assembly she waylaid Mr Lewis in the corridor.

"Yes, Ellen?"

"That accident. Is that boy really going to be all right? Because yesterday you said he might die."

"Not quite," Mr Lewis said. "I told you he was very badly injured, which I thought was the truth, which was why we prayed for him, but it was Rosalind – Mrs Bean – who rang the school, and she was very shocked. She was at the hospital and she'd run this boy down herself. It looked bad, but it wasn't nearly as bad as she thought it was."

"So he really won't die?"

"Not from this. Why are you so concerned, Ellen?"

How could she say, *Because Kasey Carter thinks it was her fault?* "Oh, I just kept thinking about it…" she said, and Mr Lewis seemed satisfied, but he was looking at her curiously and she knew it would be unwise to do anything today that would make him more curious or, indeed, suspicious.

Who could have thought that crabby Mrs Bean would have a name like Rosalind?

At home time she was first out of the door, out of the gate, and ran down the hill to cut across the fields to The Estate. It was only as she passed her own front gate that she skidded to a halt. What had she promised Mrs Sayer? Kasey might need to know the news urgently, but if the fearsome career of Calypso, the lady

146

with iron bones, was to be halted, Mrs Sayer had to know first. She opened Mrs Sayer's gate, climbed her steps and rang the bell in the front porch.

It was another first. She had never entered Mrs Sayer's front garden before, never stood in her porch. It was like an open-sided room, bigger than their kitchen in the flat, with plants in heavy clay pots standing round the edges. Ellen had never even bothered to look at Mrs Sayer's porch from the road. It had brick pillars with creepers twining up them, red tiles on the floor and rows of geraniums in planters on the low brick walls. In one corner was someone who looked very like the lady, about the same height, but holding her seashell on her head, the way people carry water. She had no lichen scabs and her iron bones were entirely out of sight.

"Arethusa," Mrs Sayer said, opening the door behind Ellen.

Ellen was reading this on the pedestal. "Who was she?"

"Another nymph. They used to stand one each side of the path until Calypso had her accident."

"Her leg? What happened?"

"My son, his friend and a cricket ball. Now what about that other accident? I suppose that's what you've come to tell me?"

"It's all right," Ellen said. "I'm just going

147

round to tell Kasey – she wasn't at school. I expect she's still feeling ill. The boy on the bike was wearing a helmet. He isn't that badly hurt after all; he broke his leg."

"Like Calypso. And what are you going to tell Kasey?"

"That he's going to be all right."

"And then what?"

"What?"

"What are you going to do after you've told her? Think, Ellen. What will Kasey do?"

Ellen thought. "She'll want to thank the lady for making it all right."

"Exactly. It'll be no good saying that the boy ran into the car because he was fooling around – I'm only guessing but I bet he was. It'll be no good saying, 'He was wearing a helmet because he's got a sensible mother with enough money to buy him a good one.' You can say all those things, but what will Kasey do? Thank the birdbath. *Pay* the birdbath – in return for not wanting a human sacrifice."

"Kasey never—"

"Kasey wanted something horrible to happen to Mrs Bean and thought some innocent boy had to die to make it happen. That's what I call human sacrifice."

"But now she knows he didn't die – well, she will when I get round there."

"Exactly," Mrs Sayer said. "And she will be wild to come round here and give her idol a present. Ellen, the lady has got to go back to being a garden ornament before she has a chance to do any more good or evil. Look at Arethusa, there. Does she look as if she could work miracles?"

Ellen looked. Arethusa had the same girly simper as Calypso, the same knowing eyes, but she was standing in a front porch in broad daylight with a flower pot full of yellow calceolarias on her head and two empty milk bottles at her feet.

"No," Ellen said.

"See what I mean?" Mrs Sayer said. "A nice, hard-working girl, minding her own business, but if she ended up in a grotto with people praying to her, she might get ideas above her station too. Now, go and tell Kasey your good news and promise her anything – short of human sacrifice. Then you and I must lay plans."

The Carters lived near the edge of The Estate in a cul-de-sac called Nettlebed Close. Ellen, approaching, felt guilty at the thought of how few times, in all the while she had known Kasey, she had ever been round to her house. In the early days they had both been too young to be allowed out alone, but recently she could have dropped by easily and knew, shamefully, that she had been avoiding unhappy Mrs Carter, silent Kray. Easy to feel sorry for Kasey now. Would it have been so hard to have done something about it sooner? Easy to walk up the path now and knock at the door, because Kray was making a fresh start and Lyndsay Carter was up and about and Ellen had good news for Kasey. Would it have been so easy if things had been as they usually were? No, but she ought to have done something about it.

The door opened and Kray stood there, looking down. If Mrs Bean reminded her of the Statue of Liberty, Kray was more like the Empire State Building, with King Kong on top.

"Yes?" he said and then, fumbling for her name, "Eileen?"

"Ellen."

"You come round after Kase? She's in bed, some sort of bug. I shouldn't get too close, you'll catch it, otherwise."

"I'll stand in the doorway," Ellen said, knowing that this was something she could not possibly catch from Kasey now.

"Go on up," Kray said, and closed the door behind her. As she started up the stairs he went into the kitchen and, through the open doorway, she caught sight of Mac, on his hind legs, making a train out of onions along the edge of the table top.

Kasey's bedroom door was ajar, so she did not have to knock, but she hovered outside on the landing, wondering what to say. Hullo, Kase? If you did not know it was spelt with a

K it would sound strange, but the way Kray had said it made it sound affectionate.

"Kase?"

She pushed the door open a little farther. The room was not large but the curtains were drawn and all she could see was the bed, with its duvet bundled into a rounded heap in the middle. Kasey had drawn in her arms and legs and head like a hibernating tortoise. Ellen went over and prodded the tortoiseshell. "Kasey?"

Kasey's dishevelled head appeared from the wrong end, as if she had turned round inside the shell. She started when she saw who it was and her face fell.

"What's happened?"

"Nothing." Ellen sat down on the bed. "It's all right, that boy isn't going to die. He broke his leg, that's all. Mr Lewis told us. He was wearing a helmet."

Kasey tried to take it in. "Mr Lewis was?"

He had been, of course, but Ellen did not want to complicate matters. "No, the boy. Mrs Bean thought she'd hurt him really badly when she rang up yesterday."

"You're sure?"

"Really," Ellen said. "So it's not your fault. Mrs Bean had a fright, that's all. And minor injuries, Mr Lewis said."

Kasey sat up and shook her hair aside. "I've just been saying, over and over, please make it all right."

Ellen guessed what was coming.

"Have you been keeping those candles alight?"

"Yes."

"I'll come over this evening."

"But you don't have to, now."

"I do. I got to *thank* her, haven't I?"

The bedroom door opened and Mrs Carter stood there. "Oh, Ellen, didn't Kray tell you? Kasey's got a bug. Don't you go catching it."

"I'll be fine," Ellen said. Mrs Carter looked very tired, leaning against the doorpost, but not really ill; a lot healthier than Kasey did.

"Well, maybe, but I don't want your mum complaining I let you get infected. And you're not going anywhere, Kase."

"But I'm all right now," Kasey protested. "I feel better."

"Don't start arguing." Mrs Carter sounded tired, too. "You've been sick, you haven't eaten anything since yesterday and you look like something the cat brought in."

"Oh, thanks a bunch." Kasey said.

"That's enough of that. Ellen, don't hang around; whatever she's had, you don't want it. If it wasn't gone tomorrow I was taking her down the health centre. Kasey, if you feel better go and have a good wash and I'll straighten the bed."

She drove them out, Kasey to the bathroom,

Ellen to the stairhead.

"TCP," Mrs Carter said, just like anyone's mother would. "Gargle."

It was a quarter to five. Mum would be back soon. Ellen bounded down the stairs.

"Kasey can ring you this evening," Mrs Carter called, over the banisters.

Ellen managed to reach home before Mum, sprinted upstairs and went to the telephone. Mrs Sayer answered immediately.

"Have you told her? How did she take it?"

"She wanted to know if I'd kept the candles going."

"And when is she making her next visit?"

"She wanted to come this evening but her mum won't let her out. She thinks she's got something infectious. She thinks I'll catch it."

"Are you sure you haven't?"

"Yes," Ellen said. "Quite sure."

"Hmm," Mrs Sayer said, at the other end of the line. "I'll be doing some weeding this evening should you be passing through the end of my garden around seven o'clock. Ah ... your mother has just wheeled her bike past my gate. Does she know about any of this?"

"No."

"Just as well, perhaps. I'll see you later."

Ellen hung up in time to see Mum opening the gate, and put the kettle on, scrambling to get the mugs and biscuits laid out.

Once or twice during the next couple of hours she looked out of the back window and saw no one in Mrs Sayer's garden. At seven o'clock, when Mum settled down to watch the news, she went downstairs and along the path by the hedge, feeling as if she were doing it for the last time. There seemed to be no one on the far side of the hedge when she went through, but someone had been there, someone who had no fear of leaving footprints and other traces. Even so, she had a surprise when the ivy curtains parted and a man stepped out.

He jumped too, but not so much, and he did seem to be expecting her.

"Ellen?" he said.

"Is she there?" Mrs Sayer's voice came from beyond the rubbish heap, followed almost at once by Mrs Sayer. "This is my son Nicky," she said.

He was the man Ellen had seen before, the one who mowed the lawn. He looked rather old to be called Nicky, Ellen thought, at least as old as Mr Lewis. He was much taller than his mother and wore jeans and a work shirt; old boots; dressed for heavy labour.

"Hello," Ellen said.

"Hello again," Nicky said, although he had not said it the first time. "Well, let's get her out, Ma. I can't do anything in there."

Ellen did not know what he meant until Mrs Sayer took hold of a bunch of ivy fronds and held them aside. Nicky turned, seized something and twisted it. Out of the grotto came the lady with iron bones, rolling on her pedestal as if it were a wheel, while Nicky rotated her head. She left a crescent-shaped track in the grass.

When she was well clear of the ivy he set her upright and she gave him her sly slanty smile upwards, *Well, hello, handsome.* There was nothing mysterious about her now.

"What do you think?" Mrs Sayer said.

Nicky ran his hand down the iron shin. "Piece of cake. I don't know why I didn't do it ages ago."

"Out of sight, out of mind," his mother said tartly. "Don't you remember how she got like that in the first place?"

"That was Charlie Jagger," Nicky said.

"It was your cricket ball."

"Well, it won't take long, at any rate."

"What are you going to do?" Ellen said. "You're not going to break her up?"

"Didn't I say I wouldn't?"

"You said you wanted to."

"And how would you tell Kasey if I did? No, we're going to disarm her."

"I'm going to mend her," Nicky said. "Slap on a bit of concrete, rub down, make good."

"And then she's going in the front porch with Arethusa, one each side of the door, out of harm's way. I've got a nice clump of *jovibarba* that will do very well in that seashell; house leeks. Ellen, there's a wheelbarrow up by the pear tree. Bring it down, will you?" Mrs Sayer said.

Ellen went round the rubbish heap and up the path between the lavender and roses. She did not need to ask why they were going to repair the lady with iron bones. Out of her grotto, away from the ivy, in daylight, she looked as she had done when Ellen first came face to face with her those two long years ago; rather silly with her smirking smile and her flirty eyes. Also, Ellen noticed, as she came back with the wheelbarrow, her head was too small for the rest of her.

"Now, you'll have to help here," Mrs Sayer said. "I can't rely on my leg. You hold that barrow good and steady." Ellen did as she was told, and Nicky Sayer worked his fingers under the pedestal, gripped the lady firmly round the neck with his other hand, and swung her upwards, over, into the barrow.

"Oh," he said.

The lady was lying in the barrow, holding her shell. Nicky slowly raised his hand. In it was the lady's head, which he was clasping by the bun of hair. In the barrow the lady ended at the shoulders, from which protruded her iron spine.

"I said disarm her, Nicky, not behead her," Mrs Sayer remarked.

156

Nicky held up the head and investigated under its chin with his fingers. Bits of concrete neck dropped off and fell at his feet.

"Frost damage," he said. "Poor girl."

"How could frost do that?" Ellen said, half appalled at the lady's sudden decapitation.

"She must have been cracked around the neck, water got in and then froze. This probably happened last winter. How long has she been out here, Ma?"

"The unpleasantness with the cricket ball would have been at least twenty years ago."

"Yes, but she's older than me. She's been out here since – when did you and Dad move here?"

"In 1949 and she wasn't new then."

"Fifty years," Nicky said. "I think she's done quite well, considering." He was interrupted by a muffled clunk. They looked in the wheelbarrow. The lady's elbow, which had once supported Ellen's bracelet, was lying at the bottom. It was only the back of her elbow, the front was still attached, but the fallen piece had a deep rusty groove where it had fitted around the iron bone.

"She's disarming herself," said Nicky.

Ellen stared at the little trickle of sandy grit that was leaking out of Calypso from some unseen fracture, into the bottom of the wheelbarrow. Mrs Sayer had been right. Ellen could never have told Kasey that the lady had been

157

broken up on purpose, but what could she tell her now?

"I wonder if we could get the seashell off in one piece," Mrs Sayer was saying, heartlessly.

There came an agonized howl from the fence. "*What are you doing?*"

They all spun round, and there in the gap stood Kasey, mouth open, hands clenched, eyes staring. Nicky, still clutching the head, put his hands behind his back like a Year 2 caught pinching Plasticine. Ellen could not speak.

Mrs Sayer stepped forward. "Kasey?"

Kasey nodded and then scowled suspiciously. "How d'you know?" Back on form, Ellen noted.

"I've seen you down here with Ellen – yes I have. She was also surprised to learn that I know what goes on in my own garden. These are yours, I think." She held out her hand containing the earrings, the mirror and the bracelet, like someone feeding pigeons. Kasey advanced carefully, and pecked.

"These are. I – I borrowed this. That's hers."

Mrs Sayer handed the bracelet to Ellen and lied magnificently.

"I know how much you like *playing* with her..." Mrs Sayer paused and waved a hand towards Calypso, but Kasey let it pass. "So I thought, wouldn't it be nice for the children if I mended her? Then they can light their candles and give her presents. But, poor thing, she was more fragile than I realized. As soon as Nicky – that's Nicky, my son – as soon as he picked her up, her head fell off."

Kasey gave Nicky a terrible look, the kind that made teachers mutter and infants weep. Nicky, properly nervous, shifted from foot to foot, then he slowly brought out his hand from behind him, clasping the lady's head by its back hair.

"You look like Perseus holding up the Gorgon's head," Mrs Sayer said.

Kasey turned her scowl on Mrs Sayer. "Who's Percy? What's a Gorgon?"

"Perseus was an ancient Greek hero and the Gorgon was a woman whose look could turn people to stone. Rather like you, my dear."

Kasey riveted her petrifying gaze on the lady's head, then she looked in the barrow at the rusty iron neck. The other three stood uneasily wondering what would happen next; what would Kasey say, what would Kasey do, as her idol fell apart? The lady would grant no more wishes, answer no more prayers, demand no more bribes. Best of all, she had chosen to fall apart at the exact moment when Kasey no longer needed her. She had done what she was asked to do and now she was going, without waiting around to be thanked. Kasey was free.

But did Kasey know that? Ellen could not take her eyes off Kasey's face.

"Really, truly," Mrs Sayer was insisting, "I wanted to mend her for you, but I'm afraid she's past mending."

Kasey did not answer. She stretched out her hand towards the lady and, as she touched her, the rest of the lady's arm dropped off, followed by her thigh; an extra heavy thud and most of her back fell into the wheelbarrow. The weight of the seashell swung her over and exposed the awful truth.

Ellen said tentatively, "She's got an iron *bum*, too."

Had she said the wrong thing, yet again? Kasey's mouth turned down and down, her eyebrows collided over her nose in the worst scowl ever. Ellen thought she was trying not to cry, was afraid she might scream, but then her shoulders shook and she started to giggle. Nicky, unsure if it were safe to join in, let out a stifled snort, then a cackle. Kasey tottered backwards, sat down on the grass with a bump and laughed out loud.

Ellen had never heard her laugh like that before, but it was real laughter, happy laughter. Ellen leaned into the barrow and patted the remains of the lady on what remained of her shoulder, just as she had always done.

"Thank you," she said.

"*Ellen*," Mrs Sayer said, warningly. "What was that?"

"Just saying goodbye," Ellen said.